INSTRUMENTAL

A Love Story

EJ Munro

CONTENTS

Confusion

Anne was bored, she had finished her homework, watched the latest episode of her favourite show on tv and now she was rattling around the empty house. She had opened the fridge door at least a dozen times, opened the cupboard almost as many but she wasn't hungry, just bored. She considered reading a book, something she hadn't done in a long time. Browsing the books on the family bookshelf there was nothing she wanted to read, everything was juvenile, little kids books or at least written for very young adults.

At sixteen she considered herself above those books, far preferring something a bit more risqué, something with a love interest or a horror twist.

She sighed and resumed her wandering of the house; it was eight o'clock and her parents wouldn't be back from her younger sister's swimming competition until after nine. She had already eaten the dinner her mum had left in the fridge, and the last of the ice cream.

She wandered down the hall, the plush pile of the new carpet squeezing between her bare toes. She decided she was going to be nosey, creeping quietly, she let herself into her sister's room. Being careful to leave everything exactly as she found it, she rummaged. She had no idea what she was looking for, in fact, she had no idea what her twelve-year-old sister would have that was worth snooping at, but she was bored and if she could find some blackmail material perhaps she could make her sister do the dishes for her.

There was a weird smell in the bedroom, like unwashed socks covered up with cheap little girl perfume. The room was a mess, she thought she must be an adult if she was complaining about someone else's mess!

She checked the hiding places she had used herself, under the bottom drawer of the dresser, behind the bed, under the mattress and eventually found a tiny diary stuffed into a sock in her underwear drawer. 'Amateur' she thought.

She sat down in the pressed steel chair beside her sister's desk. Flicking through the diary she had an epiphany, her sister wasn't an amateur, she was a genius. That or she was very, very boring. The diary was a journal of homework she had done, padded with boring snippets of club meetings and people's birthdays. She was convinced there was another diary, this one was a decoy!

She carefully returned the diary to the sock, making sure it was oriented the same and that the sock went back to exactly the same place in the drawer. Once that was done, she sat down and thought, where could she hide things, places that may not be available in her own room? Her eyes roamed to the built-in closet, a feature missing from her room.

She opened the closet and rifled through the pockets of the jackets hanging in there, when that didn't turn up anything she grabbed the chair and checked the very back of her top-shelf. Still nothing. She checked the shoeboxes at the bottom of the cupboard too, weirdly they contained shoes.

She was putting the lid back on the last box when she noticed that the lid was far more worn than the others, opening it again she removed the shoes from the box and instantly realised one was heavier than the other. Eureka!

She returned to her reading spot, intent on finding her sister's dirty little secrets.

She was still reading a quarter hour later, her sister had poured her soul into the pages of the book, each page filled with neat careful tiny handwriting. At first, she thought the admissions on the page were rife for teasing, feelings and hopes that seemed ridiculous but then there was an accusation and an admission, a secret that rang true in Anne's mind. It seemed simple but seeing her sister had written it down made her think, was it anything but?

Her sister wrote 'I think I am like Anne, I prefer the company of girls.' it was on one of the first pages and she had almost ignored it but then she thought, 'of course I like girls better than boys, they smell nicer and aren't... boys.'

There were other entries, young meaningless complaints about how dumb boys were but then there was one which triggered a memory, 'I was at the pool today, getting changed after practice and for some reason, I couldn't stop myself staring, I think I'm a pervert. Perhaps I should stop swimming." Anne recalled the last time she swam, it had been years ago, she recalled that same feeling, she also recalled wondering if the other girls felt the same looking at her body. That was the main reason she had not returned, fortunately, she had never been a great swimmer and no one had really challenged her about it. She did on occasion have to shower at school after PE but it was different, the showers there had stalls and there were fewer girls roaming the changing room with nothing on, enough that she could avert her eyes after only a quick look. She had always told herself that she was just comparing others body's to herself, seeing other girls breasts and comparing the size and shape, seeing which girls shaved, occasionally watching someone towel dry their hair and realising that her eyes were lingering.

It wasn't until a comment in the later pages that Anne felt she was intruding, her sister had admitted she liked a girl and had intentionally gone swimming on the weekend just to see her naked. It was less the admission, more the comment after that made her feel bad, it had said 'I think I should talk to Anne, she has had more time to come to terms with these feelings, perhaps she can tell me how to start a conversation with a girl about their sexuality without losing them as a friend.'

Anne thought about her own friends and whether she could have had that conversation, she had never imagined kissing them, but then had never imagined herself kissing boys either. She had seen pornography on the computer, hell she had likely been about her sister Kelly's age when her best friend had shown her a video from the internet on her tablet, giggling constantly. She had not been impressed, or she thought, aroused. 'Perhaps if it had been two girls' she thought, but couldn't imagine that either, 'perhaps I'm just a late bloomer.'

Realising the time she carefully returned the diary to its shoe, making sure everything was the same as she found it, then returned the shoe box to the cupboard and left the door ajar at the same angle as when she entered.

She snuck out, knowing there was no need to be furtive but it felt right considering what she had been up to.

Not feeling like doing anything else she took a long hot shower, thoughts of naked girls whizzing through her head. She dried herself on the oldest, coursest towel in the house, the one that actually dried your skin rather than simply moving the water around. Then she stared at herself in the mirror as she brushed her teeth, hoping her sister didn't ask for advice. At that moment she was considering the opposite, her sister certainly seemed to know more about her sexuality than she did, perhaps she should do the asking.

She put on her pyjamas and sat down on the closed toilet seat. It sort of made sense, she didn't like boys, saw no attraction to them. She had never sought out pornography but perhaps she should, perhaps if she looked she might find something that she was attracted to?

No, she was sure if she looked she would be caught. Her dad was in control of all the devices in their house and she knew he could see what they were looking at on the internet.

She decided to just go to bed, it was about time for her family to come home but she wasn't sure she could meet her sister's eyes just then. She retired to her comfy double bed, crammed into her bedroom that it only just fit into. She lay in the bed, staring up at the Pink Floyd poster she had pinned to the ceiling when she had been her sister's age. Naked women with body paint. Perhaps there was something to her sister's comments.

It took her hours to sleep, she heard her parents return and listened to her sister brushing her teeth. The house was silent by the time she had made a plan and settled her mind enough to drift off. She was going to ask for advice, for her sister's sake she told herself.

~~~ell~~~

She only vaguely joined in the conversation on the bus the next day, she was distracted and nervous. She couldn't help wondering if thinking her friends looked cute in their school uniform was her being attracted to them or just a normal girl thing, complimenting her friends.

The bus arrived at school and they all got out into the large carpark, it was only a quarter past eight so they had a half-hour before registration started.

"What's with you today?" Abby asked, they had been friends since primary school so it was obvious to her that Anne was distracted.

"I'm okay. Just didn't sleep well." Anne replied furtively, not fooling Abby in the slightest.

"Mmm, Kay." She replied in her best Mr Taggerty impression.

"Okay, so I didn't sleep well because I have something on my mind. It's not important, just let me deal with it?" She snapped, turning and walking away, "I will see you in registration."

She instantly felt bad for doing that but really didn't want Abby asking questions she wasn't ready to answer.

She walked around the back of the building and behind the gyms, she knew all the smokers hung out there. "Hey, know where Jo might be?" She asked one of the boys.

"The dyke?" He asked, she just shook her head and made to leave, not interested in dealing with his shit this early in the morning.

"She doesn't come here til' first break." one of the other boys called out, "She hangs out in the cafeteria in the mornings."

Anne turned and thanked him, giving the first boy a nasty look as she left she shot out, "It costs nothing to be nice." He just laughed at her.

She wandered slowly towards the central cafeteria area, for the first time pondering what it might be like if she was a lesbian, dealing with the casual verbal abuse.

Right enough Jo was sitting alone on a table in the corner of the room, playing on her phone. She was the only openly gay person she knew in the school, though she made it pretty obvious with the way she dresses and acted 'butch' as she called it, she was the only girl in school who wore trousers. Anne was pretty sure she strapped her chest too, that of she was on hormones because no one else in her year had that flat a chest.

She sidled up to the table, feeling like her heart was about to burst from her ribcage. She had never felt so nervous. 'It's for Kelly' she told herself, taking a deep breath.

Jo turned and looked at her and before Anne could buck up the nerves to say anything said "you look like you're here to ask some stupid question about being a lesbian." And turned back to her phone.

Anne gave a startled squeak, causing Jo to chuckle. "Spit it out, I won't bite." Then she looked out the corner of her eye at Anne, "unless you're into that sort of thing."

Anne considered bolting, she stammered a negative then foolishly followed up with "that I know of." Then, realizing what she had said, her face went beetroot purple instantly.

Jo stared at her, stoney faced for a minute as Anne sweated. "Right, let's go somewhere more private eh? I am sure you don't want people to talk."

She hopped off the table and strode quickly out of the room, Anne struggling to keep up without running. Jo took them up the stairs to the landing in front of the art rooms, it certainly was private, the art rooms weren't used for registration and they were a dead end so there was no chance of people walking past.

Joe sat down with her back to the door and waited expectantly. Anne stood awkwardly for a minute before sitting herself down in front of the railings at the top of the stairs.

"How do you know?" Anne started, then stopped, unsure how to put her questions into words.

"How do I know I'm a lesbian?" Jo asked incredulously. "Are you serious?"

"My sister thinks I'm a lesbian." Anne began quietly, "and I can't say for sure I'm not." She drew her knees up to her chest. "I don't like boys."

"But you do like girls?" Jo probed.

"Well, I don't know. More than boys I guess."

"Hmm..." Jo considered this, "but you don't flick the bean thinking about your girlfriends kneeling between your legs?"

"What!" Anne hissed her hand shooting to her mouth in shock.

Jo chuckled, "that's a no then! Well, what do you think about?" She asked, leaning forward intently.

"Well... I don't, I never..." Anne trailed off.

"Really?" Jo asked intrigued. "You never got horny in the shower? Reached your hand down when you read a racey bit in a novel? Sat on the corner of the washing machine on spin cycle so to speak?"

"No, never." Anne insisted, mortified. She could feel the blood pumping through her face.

Jo laughed, a hearty full-body laugh, her shoulders shaking. "It's okay, I'm not making fun of you, well not much. But you do look cute when you're flustered."

Anne stared at her knees, saying nothing.

"Well, you may not be a lesbian either, you could be asexual." Jo continued, "or a little repressed."

"What does that mean?" Anne asked meekly.

Jo scooted over and put an arm around her shoulder, "Some people just don't get sexually aroused, they just aren't interested in sex. Either gender." She gave her a little hug, "that said, my advice would be to try it. Find somewhere very private that you are comfortable that no one can walk in and just... play. Try thinking of things, men's throbbing penises, kissing your best friend... sixty nineing me!" She gave her a nudge. "See what works!" Jo got up and held out a hand, "Come on, let's get you cleaned up." Anne realised there were tears running down her cheeks. She wiped them away and accepted the hand up, Jo pulled her into a hug and held her for a long time.

"And if you find the thought that works is me, I would be happy to double-check for you." She whispered in Anne's ear.

Anne laughed and released the hug. "Seriously though, perhaps consider waiting a year or so before coming out. High School is hell and it's not like your choice of dating partners would go up. I know a total of three girls near our age who are gay, it's slim pickings!"

Anne wiped the tears off again and smiled. "Thanks Jo, whatever comes, do you want to hang out sometime? As friends?"

"Sure, come on, let's find you a bathroom."

—— *ele* ——

Anne perked up for the rest of the day, even Abby noticed.

"Sort it out then?" She had asked at first break.

"Yeah, mostly. We may have an extra for movie night this month though." Anne admitted.

"Oh? Do tell? Has the ice queen got herself a boyfriend?" Anne looked at her shocked. "Well, you never wanted to talk about boys, we all just started avoiding the subject."

"I didn't think you noticed." Anne murmured. "Can I come round your house after school? We can talk about it then?" She asked, not wanting to have that conversation in the middle of a crowded corridor.

"Sure, mum will be at work, just us girls we can do anything you want." The beetroot colour returned to Anne's face in an instant. "Oooo, properly saucey eh? I'm going to look forward to this."

Anne's mood fell briefly, especially with religious education next, why they called it religious and not christian she had no idea. It was almost bible study, what she would have given for a teacher who actually let them study Hinduism or Sikhism perhaps Buddhism.

She persevered through it though and by the end of lunch, she was back to normal, enjoying chemistry. A teacher who was passionate and eloquent in his teaching made a huge difference. As she supposed, did a subject you were interested in.

The afternoon flew past and as the last bell rang Anne's nerves resurfaced.

She met her friends in the bus, they were all a gaggle until she arrived, then there was a deathly silence. Instantly on her guard, she knelt on the furthest forward seat beside Abby. "What's going on?" She asked defensively.

"So, a boyfriend?" Susan asked from the back, all the girls giggled.

Anne punched Abbey hard in the arm. "Hey!" She said rubbing her arm, "I didn't tell them!"

"No, I don't have a boyfriend, it's nothing like that." She defended herself.

"Well, who are we going to be watching movies with?" Someone asked.

"It's not a boy, and I haven't even asked her yet. We just got talking today and I felt I should offer to hang out with her." She looked at the expectant faces, "It's Jo okay? People are kinda dicks to her and I talked to her and thought she was really nice okay?" She sat forward in her seat. "It's like the Spanish inquisition!"

"Nobody expects the Spanish inquisition!" Came a chorus from behind her causing her to smile despite her mood.

"So, a lesbian tryst? I'm just upset you didn't pick one of us!" Susan quipped from the back.

Anne twisted in her seat "See that what I'm talking about, a girl wants to hang out with the one out lesbian in school and suddenly they are dating? She's not allowed friends who are girls and not have them labelled a lesbian because of her?" She turned back to the front with a humph.

"Methinks the lady doth protest too much!" Someone else joked, Jenny, she thought.

She turned to give another piece of her mind and Susan held up her hands "it's okay, we're joking, bad taste. Sorry. Jo can join our film night, hell if she's as nice as you say perhaps I'll date her myself!"

"Sorry, just... I think this is why she looked so lonely today, I think her friends are mainly the smokers, I'm pretty sure they are all boys, and from the sounds of things most of them are dicks." She sighed. "Anyway, now that we got my news out there, what's up with you?"

─── ℓℓ ───

The conversation strayed back to normal things, school and music mainly with the girls dropping out one by one as they reached home until Abby's stop came.

They got off the bus and walked silently to the house, the red brick building looming in Anne's eyes as the nerves which had been building during the short walk reached a crescendo. Abby unlocked the door and they threw their bags into the corner and took off their shoes. Abby scampered up the stairs, Anne walking slowly behind.

She got to Abby's room, somewhere she had been almost as many times as her own bedroom, she had stayed the night dozens, if not hundreds of times. Suddenly it felt different, Abby was sitting cross-legged on the bed, the room was not as bad as her sister's but there were still dirty clothes on the floor and the bed wasn't made. She tried not to think about the colour of her best friend's undies. Even so, it felt like she was entering a boudoir, her friend's inner sanctum, somewhere she got naked.

She mentally slapped herself, wondering where these thoughts were suddenly coming from. She sat coyly on the corner of the bed.

"Oh come on, sit closer!" Abby insisted, patting the bed.

She moved to sit cross-legged in front of Abby. She found her gaze lingered on the blue bedspread until Abby grabbed her hands and said "Come on, we're best friends, nothing you say will stop that."

Anne gulped, her gaze now set on her hands where they clasped Abby's the feel of the soft skin under her fingertips, the warmth distracting. Finally, she worked up the courage to speak. "I snuck into Kelly's room last night. I was bored and thought it might be fun to read her diary."

"Oh no, she killed someone didn't she? Buried the body in your backyard?" Abby joked.

"No, she suggested I like girls." Anne admitted, intentionally leaving out that her sister too liked girls. "It made me wonder if I do." she continued quietly.

"So, that's why you went to talk to Jo? You wanted to find out if you swung that way?" Abby asked, trying not to smile.

"It sounds stupid when you say it out loud. But yes, and I still don't know." She confessed.

"Right, so no amazing insight from the random person you hardly ever spoke to? I must say, I'm a little upset that I was the second choice." She laughed, "Right, I know you aren't attracted to boys, or at least you don't lust after Van Diesel unlike most of our friends. So, are you attracted to girls?"

"Not really, I like seeing girls naked." She admitted, "but it's not like I imagine having sex with them." As she said that she suddenly imagined her and Abby rolling naked in the bed they were sitting on and her face flushed.

"Oh my god, you just thought of me naked!" Abby laughed, letting go of her hands.

"No...I..." she sighed, "you started it."

"Yeah, I guess I did. So, want to get naked and have sex?"

Anne's shocked intake of breath caused Abby to burst out laughing. "Joking! Seriously though, I'm not getting naked in the room with you again, pervert." She smiled, causing Anne to smile too.

"Jo told me to go home and masturbate." Anne said quietly, speaking towards the bedspread again.

Abby laughed, "That's an odd suggestion, why'd she suggest that?"

"I admitted I had never masturbated before." She said so quietly that Abby hardly heard her.

"What!" Abby shrieked, "Oh my god, you can't be serious? I started when I was twelve!"

Anne looked at her in shock, "Really?"

"Yeah, remember Scott from our camping trip? I woke up after a dream where I was kissing him and I was so aroused, I rubbed one out right there in the tent."

"The tent we were sharing? The tent that was so small that our sleeping bags were touching? Hold on, the tent that you woke me up shivering in even though it was warm and then cuddled up to me for body heat! ABBY!" Anne shrieked.

"Oops." Abby said, biting her bottom lip and trying not to laugh.

"I can't believe you did that. And I can't believe I find it oddly sexy." Anne teased.

"To be honest I think it turned me on a bit at the time too." Abby admitted. "Hey, we should do it together, right now. Then we could both say we were together for our first time!"

"I would kill you if you told anyone that!" Anne warned her.

Abby laughed, "That's not exactly a no? We don't need to get naked, under the covers, fully clothed, staring into each other's eyes." She smiled at the shocked look on her friend's face. "Or we could just kiss?"

"Abby, stop it." She squirmed backwards away from her friend. "It's not funny. I was being serious, I don't need this right now."

She made to get up, "I thought you might understand."

"Anne, sit down. I may have fucked that up a bit, I was kind of serious but when I saw your reaction I panicked and for some reason pretended I was joking." She scooted back against the headboard. "You know, try everything once, perhaps I might like it." There was a pleading look in her eyes. Anne wasn't convinced but she sat back down, a bit further away this time.

"I think perhaps I might just go home. This is squicking me out."

Abby leant forward, "I just thought it would be nice, best friends, experimenting. I'll drop it, sorry."

"So, what did your sister actually say to mess you up this badly?" Abby asked.

"I can't say, she just drew my attention to some things." Anne said, desperately trying to avoid outing her sister. "Look, I'm going to go home. Sorry. Don't tell anyone, please?"

She got up and headed for the door, Abby caught up with her as she was putting her shoes back on. "I'm sorry Anne, just do me a favour." Anne turned towards her and Abby surprised her by catching her lips with a quick, chaste kiss. "Think about me?"

Anne ran, she ran until her lungs were burning, all the way home, tears streaming from her eyes. 'Why did she have to do that?' she thought, wishing she had never told her, wishing she had been better at keeping her own secrets.

She got home and ran to her room, ignoring her mum's call from the kitchen. She dived onto her bed and sobbed into her pillow, deep wracking sobs. It felt like her life was over, how could she face her friend tomorrow, she felt betrayed.

She didn't come down for dinner. Her mum tried to get her down but she just lay, curled in bed, thinking over and over, round in circles about how she could have done the day differently. She was convinced all her friends would know by tomorrow. The whole school would know by the end of the day. She would be the new dyke, the new pariah the girl you couldn't be friends with because you would be labelled a lesbian too.

***

She cried herself to sleep but was woken by her sister sitting on the bed. She realised she was still in her uniform, still wearing her shoes. With a start, she also realised she hasn't done her homework.

"Want to talk about it?" Kelly asked softly.

Anne kicked her shoes off out of the blankets and let them thud to the floor. "No." She said sullenly, curling up tighter into a ball.

Kelly stroked her hair, "Did you get into a fight?"

"No." Anne muttered with a little sob. "I don't like you being the adult." She sniffed.

"Come on, just tell me." Kelly insisted. "I won't judge."

"I think I might need to move schools." Anne said, speaking into her pillow.

"Something embarrassing?" Kelly prompted.

It all came tumbling out, every little thing, the diary, the self doubt... the kiss.

Kelly was surprisingly not mad. A little miffed but Anne thought perhaps it was tempered by her pity for what the snooping had caused. Thinking about it, it did seem like karma.

"So, never? Not once?" Kelly asked, incredulously.

"Don't you start!" Anne said and threw the pillow she had been bugging at her sister.

"Sorry, sorry. Just, you know. Surprised, you're four years older than me. Hell, I do it most Sundays!"

"After swimming meets?" Anne asked accusingly.

"Well..." Kelly trailed off, unwilling to answer that question. "She's been your friend for years, you trust her don't you? Perhaps give her some dues? She may actually be attracted to you, your rejection might be hard on her too."

"She likes boys." Was all Anne could think to counter that.

"Some people... swing both ways." Kelly reminded her tactfully.

Anne sniffed and wiped her eyes. "Since when are you the mature one? And how come you know so much about this stuff?"

"Turns out I've been dealing with this longer than you. And there's books, and the internet."

"Oh Kelly, I'm sorry, I made this all about me. I had started out wanting to be able to give you advice!" She sat up and hugged her sister, she was all broad shoulders and hard muscle. "You're so grown up. When did that happen?"

"When you weren't looking, obviously."

Anne got out of bed, "Thanks for the pep talk. I need to do my homework though."

"So, not moving schools?" Kelly joked on her way out the door.

Acceptance

The next morning Anne got up really early, she got ready for school and left the house with plenty of time to walk to Abby's house.

When she got there she stood, shifting from foot to foot, plucking up the courage to speak to her best friend. The situation seemed so surreal.

Eventually, she became annoyed with herself and knocked on the door. Abby's mother answered the door in a crisp business suit. "Oh, Anne, Abby isn't feeling well, she's going to stay home today. You don't normally pick her up before school, everything okay?"

"Yeah, everything is fine Mrs Rosenberg, do you mind if I go talk to her before school?" Anne asked, knowing that Abby was cutting class to avoid her.

"Sure hun, pop up and see her."

She took her shoes off again and climbed the stairs. This time feeling hopeful that perhaps Abby wasn't going to out her.

She cracked open the bedroom door and called "Abby, is it okay if I come in?"

There was a rustling in the room and then Abby said "If you like."

She opened the door and stepped in, closing it quietly behind her before sitting primly on the corner of the bed. "Mind if we talk?"

Abby was sitting up with her knees in front of her, bedclothes pulled to her neck. "Sure." She said, not quite meeting Anne's eyes.

"What you did yesterday was cruel. You like boys and I know it, you were playing with my emotions and I didn't like it." Anne started, her speech rehearsed in her head.

"I know." Abby whispered.

"I was feeling really vulnerable." She continued.

"I know." Came the whispered reply.

"And it hurt. I cried for hours."

"Sorry." Came the tearful reply.

"Okay, I can see you regret doing it. I'm willing to forgive you if you promise not to do something like that again." Anne said, forcing the words to come out strong.

"I'm sorry. I went about the whole thing the wrong way. I'm really sorry." Abby said through the tears running down her cheeks.

"Friends?" Asked Anne, holding her arms out for a hug.

"Friends." Abby replied, leaning in to receive it.

A minute later Abby whispered, "Bi-curious by the way."

Anne pushed her away, laughing "Naked under the covers by the way!"

"So, you coming to school?" Anne asked.

"Yeah, suppose so. Didn't do the homework though, and I didn't get much sleep."

"Right, get dressed, we have about twenty minutes before the last bus. You can copy my homework, it's pretty shitty though." She left Abby to get dressed trying not to think too closely about the smooth skin of her back that she had just been holding.

"Mrs Rosenberg, Abby is going to come to school. She's just really tired." She explained.

"She'll have to hurry. I'm off to work but you could make a sandwich to take to school if you want to be nice." With that, she ducked out the door.

Anne quickly made up a couple of ham and cheese sandwiches and put them in a bag. By the time she had tidied up Abby came down, she was looking a little bedraggled. "Right, let's go." She called out.

They double-timed the walk to the bus stop and arrived just in time. The second bus was always quieter and they managed to get the back seat to themselves. Anne got out her homework and handed it to Abby to copy, also pulling out a hairbrush and some concealer. She sat behind Abby and brushed her hair whilst her friend copied the scribbled homework.

"You're right you know, your homework is awful!" Abby griped.

"Hey, you could have done it on your own!" Anne laughed. "Turn around and I will hide those black bags under your eyes."

"I'm sorry I kissed you." Abby said, "No, I'm sorry I kissed you then. I don't regret kissing you, I just wish I had timed it right."

Anne glanced at the almost empty bus, there were no students from her year and no one was looking back, she leant in and kissed her friend on the lips, a longer kiss than the last one but still fleeting. She then leant into her bag as Abby touched her lip in disbelief. "Needs some chapstick!" She proceeded to apply the chapstick to Abby's lips before putting some on herself. Abby was still sitting in shock when Anne leaned in again, kissing her a little more deeply.

"Right, now I can say I kissed a girl and I liked it." She laughed at her friend's cheesy grin. "How was the taste of my cherry chapstick?"

Abby hugged her arm, "I can't believe you did that! On the bus! Oh my god." She put her head back on the headrest and stared at the roof. "It was awesome. I'm never going to hear that song without thinking of this." The smile seemed permanently affixed to her face, the homework is forgotten, they just sat for the rest of the bus ride.

—ele—

When they got to school Anne insisted they visit Jo, so with the ten minutes they had before registration they went to the canteen. True to form, Jo was sitting alone, this time listening to music.

They sat either side of her up on the table as it appeared was Jo's norm.

"Hi Jo, this is Abby." Jo waved and threw an all too knowing look at Anne.

"Erm, we do this movie night at our house once a month and wondered if you might like to join us? My dad has a projector up in the loft and we all bring popcorn and beanbags and sit and watch old movies. It's this Saturday." Anne babbled, distracted by the thought that Jo was way too observant.

"We were going to have the Rocky Horror Picture Show but I thought you might think we were putting on for you so I thought we would ask what you would like. We could watch another Monty Python movie, the girls all loved the last one." She shut up when she noticed Jo was smirking.

"Believe it or not, I have never seen Rocky Horror so I'm fine with that. As long as the others don't mind me coming along?" She asked levelly.

"I squared it with them, they're all good. I told them you were cool."

"No pressure!" Abby said from the side.

"No, I mean... Oh God, I'm fucking this up." Anne said. "Anyway, it's Saturday night, some of the girls sleep over so you can too if you like, just bring a bedroll and a sleeping bag. Six PM, dad makes pizza so erm... bring any toppings you like."

She looked at Abby who was grinning at her, "Yeah, erm, cool, bye."

She went to get up and Jo said "Hold on." Anne stopped dead. "What's the address?" Anne let out a breath and Abby giggled. Jo got out a jotter and let Anne write her address inside the back cover.

The bell rang and they each hurried to their respective registration classrooms.

Both girls went through the day on a high, even Mrs Mackey's English class couldn't sully their mood. They kept looking across the classroom at each other and smiling, a slight blush coming to their faces.

They sat together at lunch, the cramped quarters in the canteen allowing them an excuse to sit close, legs pressed together.

"So what happened to you two this morning, we missed you on the bus." Heather asked.

"Oh, I just slept in and Anne came and got me." Abby dismissed the question. "Does anyone have any better homework for Physics? I copied Anne's but it's awful." she asked, sidetracking the conversation neatly.

Susan produced her homework, done with neat handwriting in purple ink. Susan really liked physics and she always got top marks so when Anne and Abby copied the homework they had to make sure to use a few of Anne's wrong answers. This too was an excuse to be close, Anne almost hugging Abby as she crowded in over her shoulder to be able to read the jotter.

"Jo is up for Rocky Horror by the way." Anne said as she rewrote her homework. "Just, be tactful, will you? I don't want to scare her off."

"Sure, we will be on our very best behaviour, I promise. No inappropriate comments." Susan said, "That is, unless she starts it. If she flirts with me I can't guarantee I won't reciprocate." Anne couldn't tell if she was joking but took the comment at face value.

The rest of the day sailed by, both of the girls did however almost drift off to sleep during Mr Tom's maths lecture. In their defence, so did half the class, his voice was a soporific. Abby had once joked that she should record his lectures and play them at bedtime to guarantee a good night's sleep.

By the time they stepped off the bus both girls needed a nap, the sleepless night catching up with them. Anne chose to walk Abby home, only noticing halfway that she was holding her hand. When they parted ways at Abby's house, Abby had looked furtively around before leaning in for a brief kiss goodbye. Anne watched as she closed the front door before giving a little squeal and, for the second day in a row, running all the way home.

This time when she arrived home she sought out her sister and almost dragged her to her bedroom. "I kissed her!" She whispered.

Her sister's eyes widened. "So you're definitely not moving schools!"

The story flooded out, her sister wringing every little detail from her, she didn't know how she could be so tired but buzzing with energy. "And then she kissed me goodbye." She bit her lip to stop herself from going squeeee.

"So you are a lesbian?" Her sister asked amused.

"I don't know." Her sister said with a puzzled expression.

"Oh come on! You kissed your best friend, multiple times, you liked it, you have to admit you like girls now." Her sister insisted.

"Yeah, but I don't feel like I want to jump her bones, perhaps a nice long make-out session but... it's nice but not... horny?" Anne trailed off.

Her sister pulled her own hair, looking skyward for guidance. "Well, it's a start. At least she's hot. And she shaves." She said, trying to get a rise from Anne.

Anne playfully punched her sister's shoulder. "When did you see my girlfriend naked? You pervert!" And instantly realised what she said and bit down on her knuckles. "I said that, didn't I?" Her sister nodded. "Oh shit. Ohshitohshitohshit. Are we? Should I ask her?" Her eyes were wide and panicked.

"If you're not ready to come out, don't text her. Someone will see, guaranteed. I'm surprised it isn't all-around school already with how you two are behaving!" Kelly suggested.

"Yeah, yeah you're probably right. We should be more careful. Should I call her? Would that seem desperate?" She fretted.

"Probably." Kelly answered and quickly left the room.

"Probably what? Probably would seem desperate or probably should call? Dammit, Kelly!" She cursed at the closed door.

'Hold on, should I shave?' she thought, just having processed Kelly's previous comment. 'no, I'm not planning on having sex with her.' she answered herself, 'but what if it just happens, shit stop having stupid conversations in your head!'

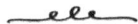

Abby lay in bed, wondering if she should call Anne. She didn't want to seem clingy. Damnit, she wanted this, why was it so damned frightening?

They had been friends forever, yesterday had been an all too stark wake-up call that she could still lose her. Just... the thought of her with someone else, that scared her more. She did enjoy it, the kisses, the stolen moments, she hadn't been sure when she started. It had been more about not losing her.

She rolled over onto her stomach. That kiss, on the bus, the risk of people seeing, the corny cherry chapstick, wow. She considered using that, thinking about it, but no. Anne wasn't likely to, for some reason she felt that perhaps she should abstain too.

She rolled back onto her back, looked at the bare ceiling, wished it contained a poster with naked bodies. Not for the poster, for the warm body that would be beside her.

She picked up the phone. Dialled all but one digit of her friend's number and paused, hung up the phone. Anne might call, that would take the onus from her.

She waited, doodling on her sketchbook, idly drawing anime characters, she stopped when she realised the most recent one looked like Anne, and that the pupils were little love hearts. She tore the page off and slipped it into her history textbook.

She gave up and did her homework, reading for English. At least it was a fun book this time, children of the dust.

It distracted her, she realised that and used it. She read the entire last half of the book.

She picked up the phone, dialled the number, almost finished when she caught sight of the time. Midnight. She put the phone down, sighed and went to bed, she lay there wrapped in the warm covers thinking about the day, almost breaking her promise to herself.

Anne had managed to stop herself calling Abby, she had also managed somehow to stop herself from shaving every inch of her body below her chin.

She had been paranoid enough about her body before her sister had crassly pointed out the difference between her and Abby, now she was obsessed. Abby knew she didn't shave though, they had talked about that years ago. She couldn't remember the reason Abby had given for her personal preference and that bugged her, she had worried the thought round and round all night.

This morning she paid special attention to her appearance, she put a pleat in her hair, made sure her blouse was ironed, she wore the silver pendant that Abby had given her for her birthday years ago. Her sister caught her checking the reflection in a window and winked around her mouthful of toast.

She waved goodbye on the way out the door and skipped, actually properly skipped, down the pavement. She was going to ask her. She had decided yesterday that it had to be in person, she had avoided phoning because she didn't trust herself not to ask, to blurt it out as if it wasn't the single most important question she had ever asked anyone in her life.

She reached Abby's house, suddenly the nerves caught up with her, she hesitated at the door, hand raised to knock. Suddenly the door opened. "Oh, Anne, you're early. I'm dashing out, I have an early meeting. It's good you're here, Abby is still moping in bed, go pull out of her pit would you?"

The impeccably dressed woman didn't wait for a reply, she flowed past Anne and into her car and was gone, leaving Anne with her knuckles raised staring after her.

She came to her senses and let herself in.

She considered sneaking up the stairs and surprising Abby, then thought she could make her a nice surprise breakfast. In the end, she just walked up the stairs, she called out to her friend and pushed the door open.

Abby was indeed still in bed, asleep. She was sprawled diagonally across the bed, her duvet only covering one leg.

Anne eeped and shot out the door. Then she peeked before she realised what a terrible thing that was to do and stopped. God, she wanted to peek though. She closed the door gently and shouted "Abby!" There was a rustle and then a thump. "Ouch." Came the reply from the bedroom.

She knocked politely, "Can I come in?" She was half hoping, half dreading Abby would let her in whilst she was in that state of undress.

"Just a second." Anne let out a deep breath. "Okay, you can come in."

She entered the room to find Anne in her nightie, something she hadn't seen in years, it was always pyjamas when they had sleepovers. She couldn't help thinking how cute she looked, and how the old nightie only just covered her bum.

She bit her lip and noticed that Abby had tidied, the room was tidier than she had ever seen it, other than the unmade bed. Abby was busy grabbing clothes from her drawers, Anne averted her eyes as the short nightie threatened to show too much, secretly wanting to look.

"Sorry Anne, I was up late reading last night and I must have slept in. I'm just going to jump in the shower." She gave Anne a look that Anne took to be her wanting to make a crude suggestion but stopping herself. She disappeared out the door without another word.

Anne looked at her friend's bed, briefly lay down in the warm spot she had just vacated and smiled. She gathered the duvet in her arms and cuddled it before getting up and making the bed. With the effort which she had obviously put into tidying last night, Anne thought a made bed would finish the job.

She trotted down the stairs, the shower was still running so she thought she might just speed things up by making some breakfast. Unlike the day before they weren't exactly rushing, her friend was not, however, known for taking short showers.

Abby stood with her head under the shower, hands pressed against the wall above her head, the hot water forming rivulets down her back, the steam had already fogged the glass walls. She sighed, knowing she had almost fucked up. Already. She had promised herself not to push, to let Anne set the pace, then the first morning she had almost asked her to join her in the shower.

She rested her head on the cool wall. Such an idiot. She picked up her razor and shaved her legs and her armpits, she paused as she was about to continue the ritual. Anne didn't shave, she knew that. Perhaps she should stop. But then it would itch. And what if they... you know... whilst it was all horrible and stubbly. Ick.

She ran her fingers over it, she liked the smooth feeling, perhaps having it stubbly would help with her other promise. She snatched her hand away as if it were burned, remembering she wasn't allowing herself. She resolutely put away the razor and finished washing her hair.

ele

Anne smiled as she saw Abby come down the stairs, her hair was still damp and her blouse was untucked. She held a chair out for her friend and pushed it in as she sat.

"Breakfast for madam?" she joked, the tea towel held over her arm in her best impression of a posh waiter. "Might I suggest the scrambled eggs on toast?"

"Oh, that would be divine." Abby responded in a posh English accent.

"And to drink, we have this fine young fruity number, overtones of orange?" Anne continued holding a bottle of orange juice over her arm against the tea towel.

"Ah yes, fine vintage, that will do just nicely." Abby responded and they devolved into giggles as Anne poured the juice and then sat down at the kitchen table across from her.

Abby tucked into her breakfast with gusto, knowing they didn't have a huge amount of time.

As she finished and downed the last of her juice, they stood and loaded the plates into the dishwasher.

"I -" they both started together.

"Sorry, you first." Anne insisted.

Abby took a deep breath. "I wanted to call you last night. Almost woke you up at midnight."

Anne smiled, "I wanted to call you too but I decided to wait until this morning." She paused, her face becoming more serious before continuing, "I didn't want to say this over the phone."

Abby's face fell, "No, nothing bad!" Anne quickly backtracked, "Erm... I wanted to ask... "

Anne waited, patiently, a slightly worried look still on her face.

"Are we... going out?" At this Abby's face lit up again.

"That depends, are you asking me out?" she teased.

Anne took another deep breath. "Abby, will you go out with me?"

"Weeeeeellllll, okay." Abby giggled. Anne let out a little squee and gathered her a hug. "So, I'm guessing we're keeping this quiet for a while?" Abby said, "Unless you want to... you know."

Anne leaned into her shoulder and happily breathed in the scent of her raspberry shampoo before letting go and holding Abby's hands, "I don't think I'm ready for that. Not yet. But in private... I can call you my girlfriend?" she said with a coy smile.

"Of course." Abby's eyes inadvertently glanced at the clock. "Oh my god, we're going to be late!"

They made the bus by the skin of their teeth, having sprinted the length of the street. Breathlessly getting onto the bus they stumbled to the back seat again, sitting in the very corner. They held hands where no one could see.

"My sister says we have to be careful unless we want to tell people." Anne said in a quiet voice.

"She's probably right, we have been a bit careless with the PDAs." Abby admitted, "And I think you're right, I'm not sure I'm ready for... that."

"She says we shouldn't say things in text too, she thinks people read our phones too often." She said, personally thinking that was a bit paranoid.

"So, sexy phone calls only? I can do that." Abby wiggled her eyebrows then she processed what they were talking about. "Hold on. You told your sister!" she said, shocked.

"Well, when I ran out the other night we had a big talk. I admitted to reading her diary and stuff. It was a whole big sobbing mess." She explained. "Then when I came in super happy the next day, well. She would have worked it out."

Abby closed her eyes. "Well, a secret is only a secret if only two people know it and one of those is dead I suppose."

"That's not quite the Mark Twain quote." Anne teased.

"Yeah, look I don't mind. I suspect it will 'come out' at some point anyway. Eh?" She gave her girlfriend a quick one-armed hug.

"Ahh, yeah, I suspect Jo knows too." Anne said, causing Abby's head to whip around.

"How! I know you didn't see her again yesterday, and we didn't say anything in the morning. She wasn't in any of our classes yesterday. How could she know?" she said in disbelief.

"She's weirdly observant. Like, spooky psychic knows what you're about to say observant." she said, remembering their first conversation.

Abby dug her Chapstick out of her bag and put some on her lips. Anne looked around the bus and wagged her eyebrows at her.

"No. We just finished saying we were being careful. You can have some lip balm if you want but," she lowered her voice, "I'm not kissing you in the backseat of the bus, not every day anyway."

Abby laughed and accepted the balm, applying it quickly, enjoying the way it reminded her of the kiss. "It almost makes me want to out myself just so we can." she joked quietly.

Friendship

The week flew past, before any of the girls knew it, Saturday had arrived. They had done this every month for years, in fact probably since they had been Kelly's age, but this time Anne was flustered. She wanted everything to go well, didn't want her stupid friends to put their foot in it with Jo, she wanted everything to be perfect. She had tidied the loft room three times, tidied her bedroom too, she had vacuumed the whole house, to her mother's pleasure. She had harassed her father about pizza dough so much that he ended up making her do it. She had lit the outdoor pizza oven herself too, it was at least an hour early and wasting wood according to her father.

She stood in the kitchen, wringing her hands, and wondering what she was missing.

"Honey, why don't you go collect Abby? You've got everything ready, relax for a bit." Her mother said, rubbing her back.

Anne looked around the kitchen again, "Yeah, okay. She can tell me what I've forgotten." she said and pulled on a hoodie.

"That's not what I meant, and you know it." her mum laughed as she left the house.

She walked slowly, knowing there was no rush as there were hours to go before people arrived. She secretly hoped that only Abby would sleep over this time, she knew that wouldn't happen though, the sleepovers were people's favourite part of the evening.

She walked past the perfectly manicured lawns; people had been out all day mowing them in the beautiful weather. She knew that because her neighbour had woken her with his petrol mower at an ungodly nine am, on a weekend! What did the man need a petrol mower for? He had about three square meters of lawn!

She passed a huge bush with beautiful big pink flowers and, after looking around furtively, stole one. That small act of theft ballooned as she walked down the street and she soon had almost a dozen flowers of all colours. She hadn't started out to steal all of them but they were all so pretty, and there were so many of them, no one would miss one. One elderly woman saw her carrying her little posie and snipped one of her own flowers and handed it to her with a smile. "It's a nice little collection, giving them to anyone special?" She asked.

"Erm, just a friend" she stammered, wondering how the old woman would react if she told her it was for her girlfriend. "Thank you, it's a beautiful flower."

"You're welcome dear, enjoy the lovely day." The old lady sent her off.

She arrived at Abby's house and knocked on the door, holding the flowers in both hands in front of her.

Abby's mum answered the door. "These are for Abby, do you have a vase?" She asked, holding out the little bouquet.

Mrs Rosenberg frowned, "it's not her birthday you know!" She said, accepting the flowers.

"I know but they were just so pretty." She said following her in.

Abby's dad was sitting at the table reading the paper with a cup of coffee, "Oops, found some pretty compost?" He joked, "morning Anne, fancy a coffee whilst you wait for Abby?"

"Erm, sure. Thanks Mr Rosenberg." She answered, sitting down at the table. "Anything new in the world?" She asked, indicating the paper.

"There's a new jaguar that no one could ever afford. The middle east is in crisis, Americans are protesting, the royal family are squabbling." He finished fiddling with the espresso machine and retrieved the milk whilst the coffee poured. "So, I guess nothing new. You aren't one of these people that insist on hot frothy milk, are you?"

"No sir, I like it to cool the coffee so I can drink it." She responded.

Abby's mum placed a little vase with the flowers in the middle of the table. "I chopped the stems, but I don't have anything to put in there to keep them fresh."

Anne fished a copper coin from her pocket, "I heard having a copper coin in there helps." And she dropped in the vase.

"I did hear that somewhere, interesting to test it out." She swept past and shouted up the stairs "Abby, don't keep your friend waiting."

Anne sipped her coffee, thanking Mr Rosenberg for it. It was strong and smooth, just how she liked it.

"Abby's been looking forward to this all week, she's more excited about movie night than I've seen her in years." He commented.

"Yeah, I'm excited too, it's Rocky Horror so it should be fun."

Mr Rosenberg's eyes narrowed. "Isn't that an R18 title?"

"It's M rated so 'Mature audiences sixteen and up'" Anne defended the choice before realising he was messing with her.

"Like we care! You watched Alien last year, it can't be worse than that!"

"No sexual content in that one dear." Mrs Rosenberg chipped in.

"You mean Ripley in her undies didn't count? I would say that was far hotter than Rocky's gold shorts!" They all chuckled and Abby mum said, "I will give you that one."

Abby appeared in a thunder of feet down the stairs, she was heavily laden with a backpack, bedroll and sleeping bag. "Hey, sorry I didn't hear you knock. Nice flowers mum."

"Anne brought those for you. Say thank you." Her mum instructed her.

She gave Anne a quick awkward hug, sleeping bag in one hand and bedroll in the other. "Thanks, I love them," She bent over and sniffed the flowers, "they smell wonderful."

"Right, got everything?" Her mum asked, "Toothbrush? Clean knickers?"

"MUM!"

"I will take that as a yes," her mum smiled, obviously winding up her daughter. "If Anne has finished her coffee you can bugger off. Your dad and I are going into town and then we have a party tonight so we won't be back until late. Be good. Don't get chucked out and no spiking the punch." She said ruffling Abby's hair whilst she couldn't defend herself.

Anne laughed and downed the last mouthful of coffee. "Come on, your parents obviously want some 'alone time'" she said, steering Abby out of the door by her backpack.

"Ew, TMI Anne!" She complained.

Anne laughed and took the sleeping bag from her friend. They walked back slowly, enjoying the sun and the relative privacy, not quite trusting it enough to walk hand in hand. They critiqued the lawn mowing and the choices of colour for people's flower beds as if they were Olympic sports, very few getting over 7.5.

By the time they returned the fire needed more wood, her dad admittedly may have been right.

"Hi Jane," Abby greeted Anne's mum. Both of her parents liked the kids to use their first names, they claimed it made them feel less old.

"Abby, do me a favour and drag Anne up to her room, she's fretting." Abby gave Anne a devious looking grin. "Sure thing Jane."

She led Anne upstairs by the hand, once they were in the bedroom she stood with her back to the door with that same grin. "Now, what could we possibly do to pass the time?" She prowled around the bed, Anne backing away playfully, then she pounced and tackled Anne to the bed, she was just covering her neck and face with little kisses when the door opened and they jumped apart with guilty expressions on their faces.

It turned out to just be Kelly, though that may have been worse, "I knew it! When I heard mum say that I thought 'they're off to snog!' and you were too! Man, you're so lucky." She jumped on the bed and said, "don't let me stop you, carry on!"

"Kelly, we're not kissing with you here." She sat up properly. "Anyway, we were just messing around, we weren't kissing, not really."

"Not yet." Abby admitted.

"Jeez Anne, you're so lucky, you find out you like girls and two days later you're dating your best friend. How can't I have a best friend who's into girls!"

"What?" Abby said, looking confused between her and Anne.

"Oh wow, you didn't tell her? Damn, I feel dumb now, I felt for sure she would tell her best friend."

Anne's face was beetroot again and she was avoiding eye contact.

"I think Anne wanted to let you tell me Kelly, so, how about you start from the top?"

Kelly shuffled closer so that she was facing Abby, who was still lounging sideways on the bed. "So, it began with my nosy sister reading my diary." She looked at Anne who was looking decidedly guilty.

"It turns out me admitting I like girls made her jealous and she decided to be cool like me." She tapped her lip with her index finger. "That's pretty much it. There was stuff about us both being perverts and stuff but, yeah, that's mainly it."

"Well, unfortunately, I don't have much experience with lesbian relationships to offer you." Abby said, adopting her own thinking pose. "You could try Anne's personal wank advisor."

"Abby, shut up!" Anne said and hit her with a pillow.

"Sorry, I meant the only experienced lesbian either of us know, who just happened to recommend Anne go home for a wank." She ducked as the pillow slammed down on her head again.

—ele—

The girls arrived in ones and twos over the course of half an hour, by the time Jo arrived Anne's dad Pete had put the first of the pizzas in the outdoor oven. A couple of the girls were keeping him company.

"Hey, Susan. Who's the boy?" He nodded through the window, "the Curt Cobain lookalike, I didn't say Anne could have boys over tonight."

Susan peered through the window. "Oh, that's Jo. She just dresses like a guy."

"Ahh, trans?" He asked knowingly.

"Nah, just butch, I think." She looked again, noticing how Jo did actually look a bit like the Nirvana frontman now that it had been pointed out. "At least I hope, we all call her... her. Hmm." She trailed off.

"Anyway, the first pizza is ready. Grab a board."

Susan grabbed a chopping board from the side and Pete slid the pizza off the paddle. She cut the pizza with the cool rocky two-handled knife thingy and handed the board to her friend Lucia. "Fancy sharing that around?" She asked, tactfully getting her to leave.

"So, Mr- erm. Pete, Anne was really clear we had to be tactful around Jo tonight, no gay jokes and no asking awkward questions. I'm sure she would appreciate that from you too."

"Hey, I will have you know I am the epitome of tact!" He waved her away, "Go play with your little girlfriends."

She smiled but didn't leave, she liked hanging out with Pete, he and Jane treated them all like adults.

Heather appeared carrying the empty board, "Mrs Jane says can you put on the prawn one now?" Susan and Pete shared a snigger.

"You go tell Mrs Jane that Mr Pete says butt out, it's not your party and teenagers don't like prawns." He said with a laugh.

"Hey, keep the peace, I'm sure some of us like prawns, if no one else I'll have a slice." Susan said, playing peacekeeper.

"Fine! I draw the line at blue cheese though!"

"I will have you know, I like blue cheese too." Susan quipped, "but I will accept that I'm likely the only one!"

The prawn pizza did the rounds, surprisingly with some popularity, if Pete hadn't nicked a slice before it went inside he would have been out of luck.

Eight girls caused a surprising amount of noise though, enough that Jane eventually left the kitchen and joined her husband outside. "At least they're having fun." She said to him, wiping soot from his nose.

"I'm just impressed they're including Kelly, I guess she's growing up eh?" He said, turning the last pizza. "And what about these pizza bases? Anne did a fine job on the dough."

They turned and looked through the window, Jane putting her arm around his waist. "I think we did well raising them."

The girls all chatted and danced to music until eight, then they filtered through the bathroom changing into their sleepwear and climbed the ladder to the loft. Pete had done his duty and ferried all the sleeping bags and beanbags up after the pizzas were done. The place looked like a hipster coffee house. Amazingly the adults had let Kelly join them, they had seen the film years ago and didn't feel any of the content was beyond Kelly's maturity.

Kelly herself was bouncing with excitement, never having been included in movie night before. Her mother had sternly warned her, "No talking through the movie!" Before sending her off to change.

They must have had a cubic meter of popcorn between them and what seemed like gallons of fizzy juice.

Kelly was the last up the ladder and she pulled it up and shut the hatch behind her. "So, truth or dare, spin the bottle or sexy pillow fights first?" She joked, only to be pelted with a half dozen pillows. All the girls laughed as she sat down.

Her sister got the DVD from Mae, the little Chinese girl was by far the quietest of the group and didn't even go to their school. She probably had originally been included only on the merit of being Heather's best friend. Her choice of movie certainly had surprised them.

The instant the DVD went on, however, it became obvious she and Heather had watched it a million times, they knew the words, not just to the songs but the dialogue too. The 'what was that bang?' line being said in triplicate had them in stitches.

Anne had been worried the floor might give way during the rendition on time warp! The girls got really into it and she and Abby used the collapsing bit at the end to accidentally end up with Anne's head in Abby's lap. They stayed that way for a few songs, no one noticing the intimacy in the excitement.

When the film ended the girls were all still hyped and wanted another film, it wasn't even ten so they found a film from her dad's collection, a silly old kids film which they all agreed on, time bandits.

Only Kelly and Anne had seen the movie and the rest of the girls loved it. It fit their old movie night theme perfectly. At the end of the movie, they left the lights down low. "Right, two newcomers this month for the first time ever!" Anne began, "We all know the ropes but these two, actually no, Kelly knows. Jo might need an explanation." She held out a cloth bag, "each person writes down a movie. It has to be pre-millenium, you have to own or be able to obtain it and it has to be a classic, otherwise no rules. We all put one in and the last person whose film we watched picks one out." She grabbed a pad and pen, " if you didn't write one down, have a think and grab the pad."

"I still think it's rigged!" Susan called out, as she did every month. "How can I go two years putting in the same film and not have it picked!" She pouted.

"The bag knows, the bag picks!" Lisa said like it was a mantra.

"The bag knows!" The rest parroted. This had obviously been a running gag.

"Hey, the man who fell to earth is a classic!" She started then the other girls finished "it's got David Bowie in it!" They all laughed and put their movie choices into the bag.

Mae put her hand in the bag and fished out a piece of notepaper, "drumroll please!" The girls all drummed on the ground, probably annoying the hell out of the adults downstairs. "Oh my god! The Man Who Fell to Earth!" She held up the paper and showed it to everyone.

"Right, it's almost midnight. If we want to continue being allowed to do this, teeth and bed. Kelly, are you staying here tonight or in your own bed?" Anne asked, taking charge of her party.

"Here." Came the reply.

"Hey, Jo, how come you haven't nipped out for a cigarette tonight, I thought smokers all ducked out every five minutes for a puff?" Abby asked.

Jo, who was wearing a t-shirt and PJ bottoms, pulled her shirt up so far that the girls thought she was about to flash them, she had the most wonderfully defined abs. At the centre of her sternum was a sticky nicotine patch. "Can't smoke at home anyway so I use these." There was a chorus of 'ahhs and nods. The girls all secretly wishing they had her sixpack.

They shuffled off to the bathroom to brush their teeth, Susan made sure to go at the same time as Jo and caught her as she entered the bathroom.

"Thanks." She said,

"What for?" Jo asked, knowing the answer already.

"You wrote my film down, the ink wasn't purple." She explained.

"Well, maybe. I do like the underdog." She smiled at Susan and turned to go into the bathroom.

Susan stopped her, "Jo, I was talking to Pete today and he suggested you might... prefer a different pronoun."

"Nah, not me, wouldn't catch me wanting no filthy phallus, I like being a girl, just don't like dressing as one." She moved to leave again and stopped. "Thanks for asking though."

"Hey!" Susan stopped her again, "Want to hang out a bit at school sometimes? Just me and you?"

Jo studied her face for a minute, then nodded and closed the bathroom door.

———ello———

Anne came back from the bathroom to find Jo sitting on a stool, she had her dad's electric guitar plugged into the amp but set low enough that you could hear the strings almost as loud as the amp.

She was playing a Nirvana song, and softly singing along. Anne recognized the song but couldn't place the title, something about angels and devils. She was really good. All the girls had stopped talking and were slowly nodding their heads to the rhythm.

She finished and was about to hang the guitar back on the wall but the girls all protested, they all wanted her to continue. "Okay, it has to be something quiet though. How about hallelujah? It sounds good sung low."

She expected her to break into a rendition of the Leonard Cohen song but this was nothing like the original, or the version Jeff Buckley sang. It was soft and throaty and most of the words were different. She didn't understand it, that said, she liked it. The engrossed girls watched her unbelieving. None of them knew Jo was so good.

When the song finished Jo didn't immediately hang up the guitar, "I've never heard that version before, what was it?" Anne asked.

"That's my take on the Nick Cave song. I like it, I thought you might."

The girls all assured her it was awesome. "Anyone else play?" No one came forward but Kelly admitted, "I sing. I could do 'I wish I was a punk rocker'" she suggested.

"Not too loud, I've heard you belt that one out." Anne warned her.

She proceeded to sing a rather good rendition of the song, Jo came in on the guitar about a minute in and managed to complement the singing perfectly.

"We should do Singstar next week!" Jenny insisted, "you could all come to our house. We have all the disks!" There was a general agreement that they should do that if their parents agreed.

Jenny lived the furthest away of all the friends so they all needed lifts and her parents didn't like her having sleepovers so they would need to be collected too. Looking at the time the girls settled for bed, Anne wasn't surprised. Even after people were in bed the murmured conversations continued for some time.

Anne had no idea when she had fallen asleep but she woke with no idea of the time, the lack of windows made it hard to guess. Abby had rolled over in the night and had a hand draped across her stomach. She lay for ages, feeling the closeness of her girlfriends body, listening to the soft breathing, and in some cases snoring, of her friends. She smiled to herself, thinking of the previous evening, it couldn't have gone much better.

She heard a soft scrape from somewhere downstairs so she knew one of her parents was up. She carefully disentangled herself from Abby's grasp and quietly got up without waking her, then tiptoed down the ladder, its cold metal rungs digging into the bare soles of her feet.

She padded lightly down the stairs to find her dad making coffee. Unlike Mr Rosenberg he used a french press, Anne didn't think it made as good coffee but it was what her dad liked. He poured her a cup and said "I'm surprised to see you up, it was a late one last night." She yawned and took a sip of the slightly bitter brew, wrinkling her nose before replying, "Yeah, it was good though. What time is it?"

"Almost eight, give them all an hour and then you can make them breakfast." He put the milk back in the fridge, "Was that the new girl playing guitar?" At Anne's nod he said, "Puts me to shame, makes me think I should practice more."

"Actually, Jenny was thinking about a Singstar night next weekend. Would that be okay?" His face dropped, "Bugger, it's our anniversary this week, you were going to be staying at Abby's remember? Kelly was going to stay at her friend Val's house. Perhaps Abby's parents can drive you? I can ask them later if you like."

"I think Kelly was invited too, I doubt she would want to miss out on a party with the big girls! I wonder if they would mind her staying too." She mused.

She went out and picked up the Sunday paper from the garden. They only got the Sunday papers, it was a bit of a ritual to sit and read each section from the heavy bundle, handing the section you read to the right and reading the next one handed from the left.

They sat down together, her mum arriving a few minutes later and quietly joining in their reading, a few sections in heather joined them, accepting the last coffee from the pot as Pete put another on to brew. By the time the second pot of coffee was gone, they were only waiting for Kelly, Abby and Jo so Anne put a load of bacon under the grill and went to fetch them.

She poked her head over the lip of the loft hatch and the muted conversation stopped, three guilty looking faces relaxed with relief realising it was Anne.

"Heavy conversation?" She asked, "breakfast is on, bacon rolls or muesli are the only options."

"Just introducing Kelly to your masturbation guru." Abby joked.

"Great, well come down when you're ready." She said, not rising to the bait.

As she disappeared Jo muttered, "I'm starting to wonder whether every girl she knows is either a lesbian or bi-sexual."

"Really?" Abby asked intrigued.

"Never mind, I didn't say anything." She quickly recanted, "so, you want dating advice from me? You realise I haven't had a girlfriend in two years?"

"Okay, so how did you meet your first girlfriend, had you already come out or... how did you know she was gay?" Kelly asked.

"Well, thinking back I think I was probably already putting out a butch vibe, I wore trousers and had short hair, I wasn't big into clothes and makeup. I knew I liked girls, unlike your sister, but I would never have said 'I'm a lesbian.' I just... didn't label myself." She took a shuddering breath, "but then I met Eve. She's a year older than me. She's very much not 'out' that was why we broke up, I came out and she didn't."

"So, how did you meet?" Abby asked, enthralled.

"She sought me out, saw the way I looked and made an assumption, she kind of stalked me. At the time I thought it was cute, thought that she was just too nervous to talk to me but I'm pretty sure she was just being predatory. She worked out the times I was alone and only spoke to me then, she never introduced me to her friends, saw me at my house or alone at school but never out and about. At the time I noticed but didn't care. She was cute and liked me and, well, we kissed a lot. I got such chapped lips my mum thought I was I'll!"

"Anyway, I told my friends I was gay. She told me she couldn't be caught with a gay girl and now she doesn't even acknowledge me in the corridors." She said, fighting back tears.

Abby scooted over and gave her a hug, "I'm so sorry. People are dicks." She said whilst rubbing her back.

"And she was your last girlfriend?" Kelly asked.

"First and last." She sniffed with her head buried in Abby's shoulder.

"So, you never... you know? With her?" Jo broke off the hug and wiped her eyes. "Nope. I talk the big talk, make out that I'm this super experienced lesbo dyke and reality is, I'm just a softcore wannabee!"

She swallowed and took a deep breath. "I guess the only real piece of advice I can give from experience is about coming out." She sighed, "telling your parents is both the hardest thing to do and the easiest. At least with mine, I told my friends first because it seemed easier, less pressure. Once I worked up the courage to tell the olds, they were cool, like really cool. My friends all drifted away but my parents are so much closer now."

She gave Abby a cheeky grin "Although, you guys have a good thing going, sleepovers with your girlfriend? That won't happen once they know." She laughed. "Make the most of it."

She got up and helped the other two to their feet. "Bacon sounds good just now, I'm a bit emotioned out."

"What about internet dating?" Kelly asked.

"Oh hell no, apparently almost all teenage lesbians online are actually middle-aged men!"

COMPASSION

On Monday Jo was surprised when Susan turned up at the canteen, "whatcha listening to?" She asked climbing onto the table beside her.

"Perfect circle just now but it's on random." She said, offering Susan an earbud.

Susan accepted the earbud and scooted close, they sat until first bell, listening to music, saying very little but enjoying the company.

The week continued on a very amicable note until one of the smokers approached the group of girls, they had been standing chatting in a corner near the maths block, "So, I hear you're all lesbos now. Such a shame." He said it whilst walking past but Susan turned and accosted him.

"If we all decide we prefer girls it won't be just because we start hanging out with Jo, it will be because boys like you are such knob ends!" She approached him, a finger stabbing into his chest, "You hang out with Jo, you know she's cool, if you were any kind of friend to her you would be happy for her. So she found some girls to talk to, why would you find that so damned threatening?" The boy began backing away, Susan kept up her tirade, "It's not like any of us come disparaging you and your filthy smoker buddies, perhaps the homophobia is to hide your little boy band's real reason to exist, smoking the sausage? So, how does it feel? Having your and your friends' sexuality questioned? Nice? No, think about other people for once, and if you are any kind of friend to Jo at all, perhaps you need to apologise?"

She had backed him into a wall and he stood there with a shocked look on his face. His mouth opened and closed a few times but he said nothing.

"Come on girls, let's leave this homophobic douche alone." She left, all five of the girls following.

"That was so awesome, I can't believe you did that!" Mae whispered to her as they strode down the corridor. "I can't believe I did it either! My hands are shaking" she admitted.

—ℓℓ—

When Susan saw Jo at the canteen the next day she was strumming a guitar, it was a dark wood acoustic but she was playing it very softly. "Nice looking guitar." Susan started.

"Might look nice but it's a second hand cheapie, my mum won't let me bring either of my good ones in. This one has a bit too high an action so it's harder on the fingers, doesn't sound as good either."

She played a little finger-picked rift and Susan was amazed, "it sounds bloody brilliant from here!" She said, "but perhaps I'm just hearing the skill of the player?" She smiled at her.

Jo increased the volume of her playing and started singing,

"I am just a poor boyThough my story's seldom toldI have squandered my resistanceFor a pocketful of mumblesSuch are promises"

Susan sat down in a chair in front of her and enjoyed being serenaded, Jo's voice was clear and bright and cut through the large room. When the song ended Susan clapped and was surprised when a bunch of the other kids around the hall joined in. Jo gave a little mock bow and continued the impromptu jam session with a rendition of 'In Hell I'll Be In Good Company' a complete contrast to her last song.

When she finished that one she put her guitar away, to a few people's disappointment.

"I don't have the gravelly voice for that one but it's catchy." She apologised.

"I loved it, I thought it was really nice the way you sang it." Susan moved to sit beside her again. "So, are you in a band? Can I come hear you play?"

"Nah, I mainly just play at home. No time for a band between running and weightlifting." She said dismissively. "You'll just have to be satisfied with me thrashing you all at Singstar!"

"Are your folks okay taking you over? We have a spare seat in the car if you want us to pick you up?" She asked, assuming that her dad wouldn't mind a detour.

"That would actually be super helpful, I was thinking I might cycle but I don't like being out quite that late on the bike." She hunted for a pen, "Erm... let me give you my address and number. Damn, I think I've left my pen at home."

Susan handed her a pen, "Here you go, keep it, I have a few of them."

"Thanks, don't know what I would have done in class!" She accepted the pen and wrote her phone number and address on the empty back page of her English jotter. "Nice pen, you sure you don't want it back?" It was a rollerball gel pen with purple ink, something Susan had been using for years.

The bell rang, signifying a five minute window to get to their registration class.

"Yeah, as I say, I have loads of them." She accepted the torn out page and waved as she took off running.

As she arrived at her registration class she realised there was something on the back of the page. She sat down beside Heather and paused as she realised it was poetry.

"My heart thumps the rhythm,My feet follow the path,It seems there is one way forward,Hard though it may be.

I push on through the mud, the stones, the hurt,I chase that closest goal, ignoring how it burns,I wonder if I should or not, keep pushing through it all,I wonder what the worth could be, that keeps me moving on.

My feet keep time, whilst my mind is free to roam,It thinks of all the could have beens and all the should have nots.I wallow in the memories, of times I slipped and fell,The pain of old still haunts me now, though wounds are healed and gone.

What risk I ask, is there to me, for chasing something new,Will I fall as hard, as fast, as far, and take another with me,Into that dark ravine,Is the worth enough, to push on sight unseen?"

It was more McGonagall than Kipling but she liked it, she suspected it wasn't really about running. Copying the address into her own jotter she resolved to give it back, in case it was English homework or something.

⁓ ℓℓ ⁓

Friday finally arrived and Susan had persuaded some of her friends to come to a cafe after school. She had asked Jo but she insisted she couldn't ditch after-school weights, though she promised to pop in if they were still there on her way home. Still, she was looking forward to a relaxed chat.

Whilst standing at the back gate of the school, waiting for her friends the smoker she had berated sautered up to her. She was in a quiet spot and his manners, though probably not changed from his norm, felt threatening to her. She didn't look at him directly, hoping he would ignore her but it was futile, he was heading directly towards her. She looked around for support but there was no one nearby, her palms began to sweat and her heart beat a little faster.

"Want to know why I slagged you off the other day?" He asked, getting a little too close for her comfort. "Why I don't like you?" She didn't respond, it seemed like a rhetorical question.

"Since you had your little slumber party, Jo hasn't hung with us once." He edged closer, "She ditched us. For you bitches." Susan swallowed, her through and mouth dry.

"So yes, I thought she was my friend, seems to me she was just hanging with us cos' she had no one else. Now you show up, we're dropped." He sneered, "You may not be a lesbian, doesn't mean she doesn't want to fuck you."

"Did you ask her?" she shrank back, not having meant to say anything. "You know, gone to find her and asked why she hasn't been round?"

The boy took a half step back. "Why should I?" he said defensively.

"She might just be quitting? Perhaps she doesn't want to risk being tempted to smoke?" She asked, pressing her back into the gate pillar.

"Urg." he grunted and rolled his eyes but he turned and walked away, not out of the gate but towards the school.

She let out a deep sigh, her hands and her whole body shaking. It was so much easier to be strong when you were in a group, out in a public place. She walked over to the wall and sat down, not trusting her legs. Damn that had scared her.

By the time her three friends arrived she had recovered her composure, she decided not to mention the encounter, she didn't want to make it a big deal.

The four friends went out the gate and Susan took Lucia's arm, putting on what was possibly too gregarious a veneer to hide her previous shock.

They gossiped and giggled all the way down to the little coffee shop, Lucia knew the owner so they were regulars, the waitress knew them by name and didn't really need to take their orders, she knew them by heart. This time however, Susan surprised her by getting a short black along with her usual diet coke. Everyone at the table looked at her in puzzlement but she brushed them off, saying she was a little tired and needed it to wake up.

They hadn't been there more than twenty minutes when a breathless Jo arrived, still in her exercise gear with her blazer thrown over the top. She looked around the shop and saw the girls waving at her.

She grabbed a spare chair from a nearby table and sat on it backwards. "Susan, I'm so sorry. Brian's a hot-headed dick but I didn't expect him to threaten you. Are you okay?"

Susan laughed, "I don't know what he told you but nothing happened, really. He got a bit mouthy and I told him he was being a dick, perhaps not in those exact words." She said, talking it down.

"That's not what it sounded like, and if the tirade he came out with at me was anything to go by, well, I'm sorry." She looked at her fingerless glove covered hands. "You were right you know. I quit."

"Well done, I'm proud of you. Some of those boys seem to like you though, perhaps don't ditch them?" Susan said encouragingly.

"You know, I only took up smoking because I thought it might deepen my voice. The social aspect was a side bonus. I'll make a point of visiting them tomorrow." She stood up, "Just, let me know if they hassle you again, I'll have words with them. Well, I have to go, I just had to say sorry."

"You won't stay for a coffee?" Heather asked.

"Nah, left all my stuff at the gym, I'd better get back before they lock up. See you tomorrow though? Anything I should bring?" She asked.

"You could bring your guitar, I know my mum would be super impressed. Singstar's cool and all but when you played the other day it was so cool." Jenny suggested.

"Right, personal performance, I may have to go home and practice."
She smiled as she waved goodbye.

"So, what really happened?" Heather asked her, "And no brushing us
off."

———ell———

Susan's dad pulled up outside the address Jo had given, they had
already picked up Lucia as she lived almost next door to them.

"Are you sure this is the address? It's a terrible neighborhood." Her
dad asked, feeling out of place in his flash BMW.

"Yeah, this is the one. Hold on, I'll just go get her." She slipped out of
the car before her father could object.

Jo apparently lived in an apartment block, it was a little run down. It
made Susan very aware of their blatant flaunting of their affluence,
pizza ovens and flash cars. Jo, it seemed, didn't even have a back
garden. She ran up the stairs to the first floor and knocked on the
door. It was answered by a tiny woman, Susan wasn't tall but she
towered over her and she was bone thin. "Hi, is Jo in?" she asked,
feeling very self-conscious.

"You're her new friend, Susan, was it?" the woman asked, waving her
into the house.

"Yeah, that's me." She paused as the woman closed the door.

"It's nice for Joanne to have a girlfriend. She's been so much happier
recently" She said, leading the way down a narrow corridor.

"Oh I'm-" she stopped herself, "Erm... yes." she continued, for some
reason not wanting to correct her.

"She's just in her bedroom." She took her through a living room
which was over filled with furniture. "It's nice of you to collect her, I
don't drive you see, and her dad is on night shift." she knocked on
one of the two doors off the living room, "Jo, your ride's here." she
called. "I'm sure she won't be a moment."

Susan stood awkwardly, rocking on the balls of her feet. "So, erm... What does Jo's dad do?" she asked, trying to think of safe topics of conversation.

"Oh, he works at the power station down the road. Been there twenty years now." Susan couldn't help wondering how old Jo's mum was, she seemed old and frail compared to any of her other friends' parents.

Fortunately, Jo emerged, Susan catching a glimpse of a poster covered bedroom before the door closed behind her. She had a soft gig bag with her.

"I thought you might want this back." Susan said, passing her the page with the poem on it.

"Oh god, you didn't read this did you?" She took the page and glanced at it. "It's absolute drivel, I'm sorry to have inflicted it on you."

"Hey, it wasn't that bad. You got everything?" Jo nodded, setting the piece of paper on the mantle.

"You be careful of that guitar." Her mum cautioned her.

"I will mum, it's only going from here to the car and back." She gave her mum a hug and led Susan by the hand back along the corridor.

"We should have her back by eleven." Susan called out behind her, "Nice meeting you."

They made their way down to the car, Susan popping the boot for her to put her guitar in before getting back in the front seat.

"Thanks for the lift Mr Niche, it's a beautiful car." She wiggled in the seat, "Rich corinthian leather." Both of the girls giggled at the Deadpool quote.

They arrived at Jenny's house, Susan realised that it was even bigger than Anne's and felt even worse for Jo, they got the guitar out of the boot and said goodbye to her dad.

"Wow, nice house." Jo said. "Yeah, Jenny's dad's a lawyer."

"Come on, you have to see the pool house, it's amazing!" Lucia said, oblivious to everything she dragged Jo by the arm into the back garden. "The pool is nice but it's kind of a waste, it doesn't get used except in summer." She nattered, the other two girls following behind. "Now the best bit is the separate pool room, it's HUGE!" She said, sliding the bi-fold patio door open.

Right enough, the pool room was probably bigger than Jo's apartment, Susan was feeling really bad she couldn't imagine how Jo felt being the 'poor friend'.

Jo however was gazing around the place in awe, "Man, if I lived here I would swim every day it would be so sweet."

Kelly had found them and heard the remark, "I've never seen you at the pool, do you swim much?" She asked, swimming being a huge part of her life.

"Not for a while, no. I feel a bit uncomfortable in a swimsuit, and it's not like I can wear trunks." She admitted candidly.

"You could wear a swim shirt, loads of boys wear those. I've got one you can have if want." Kelly suggested, "I could come with you, I love the pool."

"Erm, yeah, I guess I could try that." Jo admitted, "perhaps if you come."

Anne had heard this and came over to whisper in Jo's ear, "Don't get naked near her, she's an absolute pervert!" Jo snickered and Kelly cast her sister an evil look.

"We could all go together, that might be cool." Anne suggested.

"What! You never go to the pool, I've been asking for years! Do you even know how to swim?" Kelly asked in disbelief.

"Yeah, I'm trying new things." Anne said, "Drop it, please?"

Jo gave her a knowing look. "I think we could do a group thing, maybe next week? My social calendar has never been this full!"

Jenny's parents were chatting with the other girls as they came into the main room, as soon as her mother saw Jo's guitar case she threw her arms up, "Honey, Jenny has told me so much about you, I am so looking forward to hearing you sing!" She was a bit over the top. Jo saw Jenny shrug helplessly over her mum's shoulder.

"Eh, yeah. I mean, we're all going to sing but em, Jenny did say you might like to hear me play." She said, a little bemused.

"Oh yes, I would love that, Jenny plays the piano but she hates to sing along." She turned to her daughter, "perhaps you could accompany her? She's really good, I've had her learning since she was three. Every child should play a musical instrument in my opinion, I myself play the harp. Not exactly a traditional session instrument." She hustled Jo off to the bar in the corner, "come and talk to me, tell me all about yourself, what music do you like?"

As Jo was abducted by Jenny's mum, Susan looked to Jenny with panic in her eyes, Jenny just shrugged "She's like that, as soon as she hears her play she'll say something mildly insulting about me and leave us alone for the night.

That didn't reassure her at all but as she headed in her friend's direction Jenny's dad started talking to her and she didn't want to seem rude, she nodded and made interested noises in all the right places but the man noticed that her attention was elsewhere. "Don't worry, she's safe. My wife is in charge of music scholarships at the local university, she likes to vet talented young people she meets. Worst case, nothing comes of it, best case, if she likes her and her music, she might put her forward."

Susan was shocked, she never knew what Jenny's mum did for a living, now she was nervous for her friend in a different way.

Before she could speak to Jo and warn her about the impromptu interview she had her guitar out and was tuning it.

"Okay dears, gather round, this nice young girl is going to play us some songs to get you in the mood to sing."

With that, and still with the same bemused smile, Jo launched into song. She had never heard her sing at a normal volume before, it had always been muted due to the circumstances. This time she let loose, her voice filling the room, the guitar rising to meet it. She started off with a song Susan knew well, the scientist, the way she sang it was sad and filled with longing, the guitar part didn't seem overly complicated but the vocals shone out, it seemed she hit every note.

When she finished that song Susan led the applause and Jo smiled as she moved straight into what looked like a super complicated fingerstyle rendition of bittersweet symphony. It was amazing, Susan found herself captivated, the music soared and crashed, a woman's voice fit the piece perfectly, she was so pleased Jo had played that song, it showcased her playing and singing wonderfully. It was over before Susan was ready but then Jo played fields of athen' rye, she played it slow and sad but the song really showed off her vocal range, Jenny's mum came in singing counterpoint on the chorus and by the second verse Susan had a tear in her eye. When it finished the small crowd was silent until Jenny's mum told her "play something simple and upbeat to finish."

She sang whiskey in the bottle, it was a good choice, it had a similar cadence to the last song but more than double speed and everyone knew the words, enough so that they were all singing along after the first line.

Susan glanced to her right and caught Anne leaning into Abby's shoulder, they thought they were being discrete but Susan had seen, and had been seeing, little movements during the school day, a brushing of hair off the others face, hands held when they thought no one was watching, a touch at the waist going through doors. She saw and didn't mind, they would tell her when they were ready.

Jo finished the song and packed up her guitar to cheers and claps, Susan went to congratulate her, she gave her a big hug and wondered if Anne saw those same gestures in her interaction with Jo.

ele

The Singstar night was a huge success, there were some wonderful renditions of things like daydream believer and bohemian rhapsody and there were some truly awful but amusing attempts at it's tricky and barbie girl.

The night ended with everyone belting out Black Betty at full volume, if they hadn't stopped at ten the neighbours would surely have called noise complaints.

As they left to get their ride Jenny's mum took Jo aside, "Here is my card, call me tomorrow and we can talk about university applications."

Susan hadn't managed to warn her about this so the subject blindsided her, she stammered "but, I'm em, not going to uni."

"Oh, but you must, a talent like yours could be nurtured by a music degree."

She tried to hand the card back, "I can't afford it, I'm sorry."

"Nonsense, I'm on the scholarship board, if anyone deserves a full scholarship it is you. I have seen children with far less talent get them, and that is without my help!" She pushed the card away, "Talk it over with your parents, even if you apply and don't get in, you lose nothing."

Jo walked away with her head in the clouds.

"You okay?" Susan asked, "I meant to warn you but we got so caught up, I'm sorry."

Jo shook her head as if coming out of a daze, "No, it's okay, it's good, I think." She was still staring at the card clutched in her hand.

"Lucia, would you mind sitting in the front?" Susan asked her friend.

They got in the car and Lucia nattered away to Susan's father the whole way to Jo's house, the two in the back, however, heard none of it, they were having their own whispered conversation about universities and dreams.

"I'm just going to walk Jo home dad, back in a minute."

She hooked her arm through Jo's and steered her home, when they got to the door she said, "I had a wonderful time tonight, thank you. Perhaps you and I could do something together sometime, just you and I?"

Jo smiled at her, "I could take you running? There are some nice easy trails through beautiful countryside nearby, we could take a picnic?"

Susan paused, "I would hold you back, I doubt I could run a single kilometre just now I'm so unfit."

"That's okay, we can run then walk a hundred paces at a time if you like, anything's a start."

Jo hugged her and made sure to hold on three Mississippi's past when she thought she should let go.

"See you at school?" She said and waved as she walked away, Jo obviously wondering what had just happened.

"That you home Joanne?" Her mum called as she closed the door and leant her back on it.

"Yes mum," she sighed and dragged herself to her feet. She was going to have to do an extra-long run tomorrow to work off all the coke she drank tonight.

As she reached the living room her mum asked "Did you have a nice time?" She was reading her Agatha Christie novel and hadn't looked up.

"I think it may have been life-changing." She said softly. At that, her mum looked up.

"Where's your guitar?" She asked, Jo looked around stupidly.

"Oh, I must have left it in Susan's car!" She said, her mother shaking her head in dismay. "I can nip over and get it tomorrow."

"So, what was so 'life changing'" her mum asked.

"Jenny's mum thinks she might be able to get me a full scholarship to go to university." She said with a goofy smile.

"Is that right? Well, keep your celebrations until the money's in the bank, nothing's a sure thing. Good on you if you do though, your father and I would be proud as punch." She said and went back to reading.

Jo just said, "Yes mum, night." And got up, kissed her mum's head and went to her bedroom. She sent Susan a text straight away asking if she could come round and grab her guitar in the morning and Susan sent an enthusiastic yes along with her address.

She didn't sleep though, she was wound tight as clock spring so she picked up her electric guitar, plugged in her headphones and played. She didn't pay much attention to her song choices but somehow, every one turned out to be an upbeat love song. When she finally went to bed she lay thinking about that hug, wondering if she had been right, were all of Anne's friends somehow gay?

Anne, Kelly and Abby were all sharing a bed, Kelly had insisted on being in the middle 'to stop the hanky panky' she said. The arrangement was awkward, Kelly had fallen asleep on her side, Abby had found the only comfortable position to stop her falling off the side was spooning with Kelly, who cuddled in. Abby in the meantime lost most of the blankets and was forced to spoon the other side of her sister to get enough covers. It didn't help that Abby wore that short nightie again. It was a good job Kelly was there, the thought of that thing riding up and exposing her girlfriends bare bum had tempted her greatly.

Now however, Abby had woken in the early hours of the morning in a quandary, her girlfriend at some point in the night had reached her hand across and it was sitting in a very intimate position. Not that there was anything wrong with that, in fact Abby was keen for it to continue, the issue she had was not knowing which hand was Anne's!

You see there were two hands holding her just now, one was clasped on her hip, the bare skin of her hip, fingers oh-so temptingly close. Her nightie had ridden up during the night, or been pushed up, her bare bum was now pressed into Kelly and the hand, whoever it was who owned it, was essentially holding her there.

That was bad enough but the other hand was firmly cupped around her right breast, a thumb resting on what she just knew was a rapidly stiffening nipple.

So, the quandary was, which hand was Kelly's?

She lay in the dark, in the firm knowledge that her girlfriend was touching her, thinking back to the evening, not the party, that had been fun, but brushing their teeth before bed. Kelly had used the bathroom first and Abby had gone through with Anne, they had both brushed their teeth and then Anne had instigated a kiss. Her toes curled just thinking of it. It had been over two weeks since they started dating, they had snuck kisses here and there but this! It had been the first time they kissed somewhere truly private, without the threat of discovery, and what a kiss. Thinking of it now made her wish Kelly was not in the bed, she wanted nothing more than to continue the kiss, make it last all night, perhaps go a little further, if Anne was keen.

She took a guess and gently moved the hand from her breast, Kelly made a slight keening noise in her sleep which made her think she guessed right. Now she was wondering if she should manipulate the other hand, steer it where she wanted it to go, as it were. She didn't, but only because she still had doubts as to its owner.

She woke again with light streaming in the window to find Anne had left the bed at some point, Kelly however was now cupping her other breast. She firmly moved the hand and Kelly spluttered awake.

"You're a very handsy young lady." Abby berated her, she at least had the decency to blush and look embarrassed. Abby pulled her nightie down and got out of bed, leaving Kelly to lounge.

Kelly watched her leave and thought back to the night, she may have, possibly, potentially, woken up and found herself feeling up her sister's girlfriend, and then not moved her hand. She lay on her back thinking back on this, the feeling of a nipple hardening, the soft flesh of her breast under the flimsy cotton.

Her hand strayed under the blankets and she did something else she really shouldn't have in someone else's bed.

Courage

Jo called the number. She had waited until nine, a nice sociable time, even though she had been sitting at the kitchen table holding the card, and her phone, since five. She drew circles in the condensation that had dropped from her glass onto the melamine tabletop. The phone rang enough times that she was about to hang up and then, as she took the phone from her ear, someone answered.

The conversation that followed was hard on her, apparently, in order to win the scholarship she would have to prove academic excellence in the field of study, something she could easily do. She also needed to prove a decent grade and appropriate academic effort in her other classes. She needed to show extracurricular activities, something she could easily do. Finally, she had to prove 'economic hardship' not 'can't afford to live' hardship, just can't afford to pay for university. This she found hard. Her dad was a proud man, he didn't like handouts and he didn't like other people seeing his business. She had to persuade him to give her three years worth of tax summaries and bank account statements.

She sat with her head in her hands, her mum had Crohn's disease, she hadn't worked for years and she had been constantly in and out of hospital since Jo could remember. Her dad did earn a decent wage, but he was the family's sole earner, so it was all down to him.

Her mum came in and put the kettle on. "You going to your friend's house this morning?"

"Sorry, what was that?" She had been so distracted she hadn't heard what her mum had said.

"Getting your guitar back! It's an expensive instrument, I don't want you ignoring it." She said, vehemently.

"Yes, mum." She said meekly. "Mum...?"

"What's wrong?" Her mum asked sharply over the noise of the boiling kettle.

"Do you think I could get copies of dad's income tax and bank statements for this application?"

Her mum sucked air through her teeth. "Not sure he'll like that. It's necessary is it?"

"Yeah, I can't apply without it." She said with a small pout.

"Hmmm, well, you run along to your friend's house and I'll see what I can do." Her mum patted her on the shoulder. "Run along, days a-wastin'"

She gave her mum a hug and went to get changed into her running gear, might as well get some training in on the way over.

Susan's house was a few miles away, not far enough to break a sweat over if she ran her normal pace so she did speed training on the way, sprinting as hard as she could for as long as she could and then jogging slowly until she recovered. By the time she reached Susan's house, she was drenched in sweat.

She knocked on the door and stood back panting. Susan answered and went to hug her before realising how wet she was. "Ew! You look like you ran a marathon!" She said recoiling before she entered the hug.

"I was going to ask if you wanted to come bowling but... I don't think you're dressed for it!"

"Damn, I would have liked that, I didn't even bring my wallet though." She said, meaning it too.

"You could borrow some of my clothes, they might be a bit, erm, girly, for you."

"Yeah, I could, but I didn't bring enough money. I only ever take bus fare when I run." She said regretfully, she was willing to cross-dress for a short time for the chance to hang out with Susan.

"Meh, my dad's paying. There's no way he would let my friends pay for themselves!" Susan assured her.

"Well, I'm super sweaty, I would stink the place out."

"We have a shower. Duh!" Come on, if you're willing to borrow some clothes then I'll sort something out whilst you're in the shower.

Jo was bundled into the house and up the stairs, Susan's bedroom had an ensuite bathroom which was bigger than Jo's family one!

She shooed her into the bathroom and handed her a clean towel.

"I'll set some clean clothes inside the door for you ready for when you get out. Promise I won't peek." Susan insisted.

Feeling a little flummoxed, Jo shut the door, noting the lack of a lock. She warily peeled off her wet running gear and turned on the shower. She stood self-consciously, waiting for the water to heat up in front of the huge mirror which covered the whole wall above the sink. She examined herself in the mirror, something she didn't really do very often as the mirrors at home were pretty tiny. She decided she liked what she saw, her muscles were defined and her skin glistened with sweat. She struck a bodybuilder pose and instantly looked round in case someone had seen.

The shower door started to fog up so she stepped in, it was closed on three sides so she actually felt pretty safe from prying eyes. Susan's body wash and shampoo were on a ledge along with a scrunchy shower doodad, she used it to lather up, using as little of the expensive soaps as she could and then washed her hair. She stared at the razer hung in a little pink plastic holder and looked at her hairy legs, damn she hoped Susan didn't try and put her in a dress.

She rinsed all the soaps off and spent a minute enjoying the rain head on the shower before playing with the controls, the other showerhead had as much pressure as a firehose, it felt so good on her back. She stopped procrastinating and figured it was time to find out what girly shit she had to wear.

Turning off the water she peeked her head out of the shower, making sure she was alone.

There was a small pile of clothing just inside the door. She got out and towelled dry, eyeing the pile nervously. It had been a long time since she wore anything not purchased from the boy's section.

Picking up the pile she found Susan had been thorough, there were even undies in the pile.

She pulled them out, they were white with red piping, small, hip-high with a cherry on the front. She cringed and put them on, looking again at her reflection.

'Well Jo, you know what her knickers look like now!' She thought to herself. She picked up what looked like a bra, just with no support, she set it aside with a 'nope' and reapplied her nicotine patch and her silicone nipple covers. It was the only concession she normally gave to being a girl, otherwise, it got embarrassing when it was cold.

She pulled on the white socks and form-fitting blue jeans, then she picked up the t-shirt, it wasn't too bad, still, a girl's cut but it was a well worn black REM t-shirt with gig dates on the back. She pulled it on and looked at herself again in the mirror.

Her biceps strained the cuffs of the tee, otherwise, the girl staring back looked, normal, like a girl. She cringed and sat on the toilet. She breathed heavily, trying not to give up, to run away.

A knock came on the door and she opened it. Susan was standing with a plain black hoodie. Jo grabbed it and threw it on, causing Susan to take a step back in shock.

"Sorry," Jo started, "I have... issues."

"Want to sit down for a minute? Tell me about it?" Susan offered.

Jo looked at her for a bit, then decided it might be a good idea.

She sat on the edge of the bed and Susan sat beside her, "It's a kind of body dysmorphia." she began, "I look at myself dressed like a girl and I don't recognise myself in the mirror. It's not me staring back."

She slumped back on the bed. "It's why I run." Susan slowly lay down beside her and gave a questioning look.

"Someone told me a long time ago that skinny girls don't grow big tits. I was like, eight or something. I already had this problem with clothes and I had a dread, like a proper phobia of seeing myself with tits." She closed her eyes and shuddered. "I developed an eating problem, close to full-on anorexia. Then I saw the runners on the tv. It might have been the commonwealth games or something and I thought, none of those girls have boobs, I could do that. So I did."

She opened her eyes and looked at Susan, "I don't know if it worked or if I never would have gotten them but I'm not stopping now."

"Is that why you lift weights too?" Susan asked gently.

"Nah, that's the other woman's issue. Serious weightlifters don't get periods." She sighed, "at least not many. And when I do, I just double down on the work."

"That one I can understand." Susan agreed, "perhaps I should join you!"

"You would be welcome, but I wouldn't recommend it. It's a fucktonne of work for a lousy benefit."

She got up and pulled Susan to her feet. "Let's go bowling, I can manage."

Susan smiled and gave her the hug she had missed at the front doorstep.

ele

It was just Susan, Lucia and Jo at the bowling alley, Susan hadn't invited anyone else. Her dad had paid for two games, drinks and fries and had left them to it.

On the first frame Susan threw her ball down the lane, it sailed a good third of the way down the lane before bouncing into the gutter. Her second ball wasn't any better.

"Erm, you have played this game before haven't you?" Jo asked.

"Yeah, I'm a bit shit though." Jo watched as Lucia's ball also sailed into the gutter twice in a row.

"Okay, can I give you both some pointers?" She asked, nervous the manager may throw them out for destroying his lanes.

"Sure! Anything to help me beat Heather next time we play!" Susan agreed enthusiastically.

"Okay, so when you release the ball, you have to do so from the level of the ground. Lucia did that, but she rotated the ball around her hip, which put spin on the ball and caused it to go left." She demonstrated what she meant, "now to stop that happening you have to swing one leg out behind like this."

She strode to the lane and made a graceful sweeping motion, releasing the ball without a sound and it raced down the lane, all the pins seemed to jump backwards as if scared of the ball.

"Strike!" The other two shouted and both hugged her, jumping up and down.

"Erm, yeah." Jo laughed, amused by the antics. "I get a few of those so perhaps tone down the celebrations on my goes?"

"Sorry, so like this?" Susan asked, pantomiming the motion.

"Exactly, give it a try."

Susan did a little shuffle at the end but managed to release the ball well and she knocked down four pins. She did a little dance and a fist pump.

"Okay, better but you need to know which foot to start on and you need to keep your pace steady. That little two-step you did was because you were wrong-footed. It's like the high jump." She explained. "Take a few walks from the seats to the line and see if you can work it out."

She did that and when she thought it was right she tried again, knocking all but one pin down. Again she danced and this time held Lucia's hands and jumped around.

"You're a really good teacher, where did you learn all this?" Lucia asked.

"My dad is in the bowling league, he takes me with him when mum's in the hospital."

"Oh god, I'm so sorry. What's wrong with her?" Lucia asked.

"Crohn's, it's a gut thing, they keep cutting sections out of her intestines because it gets inflamed and her body tries to fight itself." She brushed it off.

"Geeze, that must be hard." Susan said, "I thought she looked frail last night."

"Oh don't let her fool you, she'll still thrash you to within an inch of your life if you wrong her!" Jo replied, "Anyway, it's your turn, have a few practices first."

Lucia's next shot was straight as a die. Unfortunately, it was off to the left so only clipped the side pin.

"That was better! You just need to aim." She got up and led Lucia to the line, see these arrows at the line? You want to pay attention which arrow you release the ball on and see the diamonds a few feet further in? You want to aim at the corresponding diamond, it's easier than aiming all the way down the bottom and your ball should go pretty straight."

Her next ball hit the pin to the right of centre and took out another five pins, the girls celebrated this small win. "It's amazing, we sometimes struggle to get double digits!" Lucia gushed.

Jo took her shot, scoring another strike. The other girls started to celebrate, then they saw the amused look on Jo's face and stopped. "Sorry. Force of habit." Susan said with a grin.

By the end of the first game, the scores were respectable, Jo was in the mid-hundreds and both of the others had broken sixty. Susan had gotten sixty-nine and had nudged Jo and waggled her eyebrows.

Lucia excused herself to visit the toilet between games and Jo turned to Susan. "Can I have a word?"

Susan shot her a confused glance, "Sure."

Jo led her to a quieter part of the room. "Susan, erm." She started hesitantly, "You know how I'm a lesbian?" She ploughed on without waiting for a reply. "Well, I'm not sure you've noticed, but sometimes it feels like you're flirting with me."

"Well, yeah." Susan said with a sly smile.

"Well, I kind of need to know, is it because you find it fun, or are you actually interested." She had been dreading asking this question since the hug last night but felt she shouldn't put it off.

"I wouldn't flirt if I wasn't interested." Susan said, confidently.

"I'm not interested in playing around and hiding it from everybody. If we do this you would have to be all in. As in, all out. I've done the covert stuff before and got seriously burned." Jo insisted, her heart falling.

Susan paused, her face went flat for a long moment. "Can we go on that date, the picnic we talked about first?" She took a deep breath. "If we decide we are dating after that then I will tell our friends. Would that be okay?"

It was more than Jo had hoped for, she had readied herself for rejection, expected it even. She pulled Susan into a big hug, "It's a big step you know. Some people will not be nice." Susan nodded into her shoulder. "I did tell them if you were nice I might date you myself, they shouldn't be too surprised." She laughed. "Lucia's waiting."

In the next frame, they all improved on their scores and Jo joined in their celebrations more vocally.

ele

When she was dropped off at the apartment with her guitar and her little plastic bag of dirty clothes her father had already left for an overtime shift at work.

"He left those for you hun." Her mum said, pointing to a small stack of paper. "Best get them copied today before he changes his mind."

Then her mum caught sight of her clothes. "You're looking -"

"Don't, please mum just, don't say it." Jo pleaded.

"Happy," her mum continued. "Not your normal clobber?"

"Susan lent me some clothes so we could go out." Jo admitted, defensively.

"Nice for you to have a girlfriend again." Her mum said, shuffling off to the kitchen.

"She's not my girlfriend mum." She called after her.

"Well, she never denied it when I asked. Perhaps that says something?" The reply came from the kitchen.

"I'm off to change." She called, not deigning to reply.

She got into her bedroom and stripped to her undies, she ran her fingers over the cherries on the front 'they are quite comfortable.' she thought quietly. 'No point dirtying two pairs.' She left them on and dressed in her normal clothes, and returned to the living room.

Wearing Susan's underwear felt like she had a dirty little secret, she bit her lip, for some reason, it turned her on slightly.

"I'm going to call Mrs Mendez, Jenny's mum." Jo said, picking up the phone.

The call was answered on the first ring and they discussed the documents her dad had provided, Mrs Mendez was delighted she was taking the application so seriously. When she told her she was going to get them photocopied, however, she said "Copies of documents need to be notarized, it just guarantees they are original. I'm a notary myself so you could bring them here. If you're doing that you should bring a passport photo too, I can sign the back."

"Erm, are you available today?" Jo asked conscious her mum had wanted her to return the documents.

"Of course dear, pop round this afternoon, in fact, come for dinner. I'm sure Jenny would love to have company." Jo quickly confirmed this with her mum, "that sounds great Mrs Mendez, if it's not an imposition." She quickly finished the phone call and hung up.

"Well, it looks like I'm going out again! Any idea where I can get passport photos?" She asked her mum.

—— *ele* ——

Abby's parents were cooking a big roast lunch so Anne and Kelly went home straight after breakfast, Anne didn't even manage a kiss goodbye.

When they got home their parents were looking slightly worse for wear. "Good anniversary dinner? Anne asked cheerily, her mother groaned.

"She wasn't complaining at the time." Pete said, "the cocktails at the bar and the dancing were both her idea!"

"Oh god. I feel sick just thinking about that margarita." Her mum moaned.

"So, quiet day in front of the TV?" Kelly suggested, grabbing a fruit juice from the fridge. "You still okay to take me swimming."

Her mum looked at her and went decidedly green, she jumped up and ran to the bathroom.

"I guess that's a no." She said, trying hard to keep the disappointment from her voice.

"If you don't mind the bus then I'll go with you." Anne said, trying to be helpful.

Her dad looked hopefully at Kelly.

"I'm okay with that if we go early and you come for a swim." Kelly said with a pout.

Anne looked at her disbelievingly. "Really?"

"If you're willing to go with Jo and Abby you can't hate it that much." She figured.

"I don't know if I even still have a swimsuit that fits." Anne said, trying to think of a way out of it.

"I have loads, we aren't that different height wise now so you would probably fit one." She smirked. "The swim meet is at two, if we have an early lunch and leave here at midday we should get a good swim in."

"Okay, fine. You better find me a nice one though, something that doesn't show too much skin." The girls wandered off to Kelly's tip of a bedroom without noticing their dad's amused smile.

Kelly had found a very conservative black swimsuit which was low cut at the hip and high necked. Anne put it on at home, wanting to avoid spending too much time in the changing room, and to avoid nudity as much as she could.

They rode the bus, Kelly nattering on about little things going on at school. Anne only gave her half an ear, her mind on the swimming pool and their lack of changing rooms. She was wishing they could have gone to the bigger swimming pool across the town, they at least had a few changing rooms, but Kelly's swimming class was at the local one.

When they got there the changing rooms were empty, Anne quickly shrugged off her clothes and put a coin in the old locker that she had put her bag and shoes into. She was just fastening the key to the strap of her swimsuit when two girls from her year came in, wet from the pool.

One of the girls looked her way and said, loud enough for her and Kelly to hear, "look out, it's one of the new apprentice dykes, better not take our clothes off yet."

Kelly looked like she was about to say something but Anne just steered her out of the changing rooms, "It's not worth it." She said as she passed the girls, "they're just being homophobic pricks."

"Fuck off pervert." the girl who spoke shouted after her. Anne just led her sister out to the pool.

Once they were in the pool she let herself cry, the tears invisible in the water streaming off her face. She had been fine until the pervert comment, unfortunately, she did feel like a pervert. She just hoped her friends were not receiving the same treatment, socialising with Jo had been her idea after all.

Kelly swam up beside her and quietly said, "It's not like you would want to see them naked. The one who spoke has a really nasty appendix scar and her friend has a huge strawberry birthmark."

"Oh my god, Kelly! You really are a pervert! And you can't judge people like that, they can't help those things!" She was shocked but the comment had caused her to smile, her mood lifting.

"Come on, let's go to the deep end and do some diving. I'm going to be swimming enough laps later on." Her sister insisted.

They spent the rest of the time before Kelly's swimming class messing around, climbing out of the pool and doing flips and dives, swimming underwater and tackling each other. It was actually a lot of fun.

When it was time for the swim class Anne again wished they were at the bigger pool, it had a hot tub which she could have soaked in whilst waiting for Kelly. As it was she resigned herself to doing some lengths of the pool in the two available lanes whilst keeping an eye out on how many people were going into the changing rooms.

It was almost halfway through the class before she decided it was safe.

She got out and retrieved her towel from the cubby hole beside the changing rooms and headed into the women's showers. It was blessedly empty so Anne stripped off her wet costume, letting it land on the floor with a splat. The shower room was a large open room with showerheads all around the walls and push buttons to activate them.

She pushed the button and waited for the water to warm. As she stepped into the shower a woman, perhaps twice her age, stepped into the room behind her and started taking off her costume. "At least it was a nice temperature today." the woman said, obviously wanting to strike up a conversation.

Anne averted her eyes and turned her back, using the pool supplied shower gel from the dispenser on the wall to lather her hair. "Yeah, it was nice."

"You did a fair few lengths today, what did you get to?" the woman asked, she had been in Anne's lane so it wasn't so unusual for her to have been keeping track.

"I don't know, I wasn't really counting." Anne said, speaking into the corner.

"Ahh, I got all the way up to sixty. A kilometre and a half. I'm building up a few more each week." The woman said. "You're here with your sister?"

Anne looked at her properly for the first time. The woman was standing in the shower facing her, unashamedly displaying her body. Anne didn't recognise her.

"Yeah, how did you know that?" Anne asked, averting her eyes again.

"Oh, I talk to Kelly all the time, she's a very mature kid." Anne let out an inadvertent laugh.

"You obviously catch her at the right times, she can be quite immature depending on the situation." The shower cut off and Anne grabbed her towel, having washed all the suds off already.

As she walked out of the shower the woman followed her, leaving the shower running, "Perhaps have a word with her about not being so obvious about checking out the other girls. It's okay to look but I've seen her... look if you know what I mean."

"Erm, yes, okay I'll tell her." Anne said, embarrassed about the attention from this stranger.

She hurriedly changed whilst the woman wrapped her hair in her towel and took her time sorting her clothes and wringing out her swimming costume.

"If you don't want to draw attention you need to find the middle ground." the woman said as Anne was about to leave. "Don't obviously avert your eyes like you are doing, but make sure most of your attention is eye level." Anne looked at her in puzzlement. "See, that's better. If you want to avoid people noticing your discomfort, pretend to be comfortable. Make eye contact."

Anne nodded and left, going to the narrow viewing area and wondering at the strange encounter she just had.

ele

"Lucia, I don't want you associating with that girl." Her mother had been arguing with her over Jo's sexuality since she had found out that she was gay. Lucia had been born here but her mother had been brought up in Saudi Arabia, she was a practising Islamic and any kind of gay relationship was a serious taboo.

"Mum, she's not turning us all gay! She's just a normal person who happens to like girls!" Lucia pleaded.

"It is against Sharia law, it is banned in the Koran! I know your father lets you get away without worshipping, but I will not have this in my house and not with my family. You are not to see her and that is it." Her mother walked out of the room, her words final.

"Arrg, dammit! How am I meant to avoid one friend when we all hang out together! Stupid woman." She ranted to herself.

She went to speak to her father, "I'm sorry Lucy, it's something your mother feels very strongly about. Once you are at university you can do as you like but I would suggest not pushing your mother on this." Was all he would say.

Her sisters understood her frustration but were unable to help, in the end, she decided the only way around it was to lie. Her mother rarely saw her friends or their parents, surely she would never know.

ele

It was frosty on Monday morning, the end of the summer always had a few really cold mornings, then autumn would come and there would be rain and wind. School uniforms were certainly not made for cold or wet weather! Both Abby and Anne were shifting from foot to foot, trying to keep their toes warm. They were wearing their thickest tights and had their hands bundled up into the coat sleeves but the cold was biting, the end of Anne's nose felt like it was a solid lump of ice.

"Damn, why is the bus always late when it's bad weather?" Abby asked her.

"Well, hopefully it is just late, we will be waiting a while longer if we missed it." She stamped her feet and shivered.

"We could cuddle together for warmth!" Abby suggested.

"I'm already getting called a lesbian, let's not fuel the rumours." Anne said in a surly voice.

"I guess we're not coming out anytime soon then." Abby said, with a tone of disappointment.

"I don't know if I'm ready. It's a big step. It will affect all our friends too." She said apologetically.

"Hmm, oh, there's the bus!" Abby waved at the bus driver.

They showed the little red bus passes, even though the same driver had picked them up every day for the last three years, and got on the old clapped out bus.

"Why do the school runs get the crappiest busses?" Abby griped as they sat down in front of their friends.

"It's because school kids are vandalistic dickheads!" Heather said from the back row. "Come see this."

Abby got up and visited the seats two rows back. Someone had scrawled 'Homos only' on the back of the seat.

"How original." She said as she sat back down.

"To think Jo has gotten this all through high school. I know I've said it before but people are dicks." Susan said, using a wet wipe from her bag to try and remove the words.

"My mum has banned me from socializing with her." Lucia said quietly.

"What? I can understand dumbass teenagers but what's your mum got against her?" Heather asked.

"She's Islamic, where she's from they drag homosexuals into the street and stone them to death." She replied, sullenly.

"What are you going to do?" Susan asked, wondering how much worse it might be if suddenly Lucia's best friend came out.

"Well, I'm just not going to tell her. It's not like she can see who I hang out with at school." She gave a sly smile, "She doesn't talk to my friends anyway, I don't know if anyone other than Susan has ever met her. If I hadn't let slip about Jo dressing like a boy she never would have known."

"Jo came round our house for dinner yesterday." Jenny said, "It was really fun, mum had us playing music after dinner. Dad played the drums, it was like being in a band. Even mum joined in on her harp."

"Your mum invited her to dinner?" Heather asked, "she never invites me!"

"She was helping her fill out a scholarship form, she had a bunch of stuff to sign." She explained.

"I'm thinking I might apply to the local uni too." Susan said. This got a lot of attention.

"What brought that on? I thought you wanted to 'fully embrace student life' live in a student flat, miles away from your parents and go out partying, all that stuff." Lucia asked, surprised.

"Yeah, maybe." Susan said, trying to drop the subject.

"I guess you could persuade your dad to get you a flat in the city, it would be a long commute from the burbs' every day otherwise." Jenny suggested.

Susan had a fleeting fantasy of living in a flat with all her friends, going to the same university.

"We should all apply, we could all live together! That would be so cool!" Heather said, obviously having shared that fantasy.

"I don't think you get seven-bedroom flats!" Abby laughed.

"We could bunk in with each other." Heather defended her idea.

"Hey, I just got rid of one offensive slogan, don't give them more ammunition!" Susan scoffed.

MALIGNANT

Anne wasn't sure if she had imagined some of the incidents over the next week, people stopping talking as she walked past, whispered conversations whilst looking in her group's direction, people inexplicably turning and walking in the other direction. What wasn't imagined was the girl from the pool blatantly telling the gym teacher she wouldn't get changed in the same changing room as Anne. It hurt. She wanted to retaliate but had no idea how without causing more harm.

They were sitting in history, the only class where she and Abby sat together. The teacher was going over the politics of ancient Rome, it was deathly boring.

"Miss!" One of the boys called from behind the girls, "Miss! Abby's been drawing naked pictures of her girlfriend!"

"What!" Abby exclaimed, mortified.

"Sean, sit down and shut up, no more of your spurious accusations." The teacher admonished, the boy had a bit of a reputation for stirring up trouble.

"No miss, look!" She called holding out a sheet of paper.

The teacher walked down the aisle and snatched the paper from his hand. She examined it for a second. "Want to explain this?" She asked Abby.

The paper did actually look at first glance like Anne's naked torso. Abby remembered drawing figures weeks ago, she had forgotten the paper in the aftermath and it must have dropped from her textbook when she pulled it from her bag.

"It's just unfinished, I sketched in a vague outline and was going to draw in the clothes once the face was done. It wasn't even meant to look like Anne, I took it in to show her because I thought it was funny I had unconsciously drawn her." She said defensively.

"There you go Sean, perfectly rational." She left the picture on the desk and returned to the whiteboard. "Now, back to the senate."

There was a stage whisper from Sean, "I bet she's really been nude modelling for her girlfriend."

The teacher whirled around, "THAT'S IT SEAN, ENOUGH, OUTSIDE AND WAIT FOR ME." She shouted. The class went deathly quiet and Sean traipsed out.

"Okay, back to the Senate, no more snide comments and distractions. I will appreciate you NOT casting aspersions on your classmates, especially in my class!" With that, she continued teaching. Sean was left in the corridor until the end of class, at which time she could be heard yelling at him in the classroom from halfway down the corridor.

"Although I'm glad she dealt with him pretty harshly, this is going to be all around the school by the last break." Anne lamented.

"I'm sorry, I shouldn't have taken the picture to school. I didn't even realise it looked like a nude." Abby said sullenly. "Man, why is this happening even when we're really careful? I think we should perhaps wait before we tell people."

Susan puffed and panted as they ran up the trail, the weather was cool which was just as well as she was sweating so much it looked like she had taken a shower in her clothes.

"Can...we...stop...a...minute." she panted, watching as Jo came to a halt and stood running on the spot.

"It's better if you walk." She admonished, looking as fresh as when they started.

Susan leant on her knees and panted, "Just... need...to catch..." the trail they were on snaked up around a hill, it wasn't steep but it was constant. "Whoo, okay...I'm good, let's walk a bit."

The view was wonderful, they were only halfway up but the houses were already looking tiny, the patchwork of the fields outside town was visible in the dark green of hedgerows.

"You're doing great, if you need more stops just say, we ran twice as far that time than I expected you to." Jo said encouragingly, she was still jogging at Susan's walking pace. "On the way down you will likely find you hardly need to stop. Downhill rocks!"

They continued running and walking with considerably less running involved as they approached the top of the hill, Jo was carrying the backpack with their lunch in it and was making it look light as a feather. Having packed it herself Susan knew it was actually rather heavy. Along with the food and picnic blanket, Jo had insisted she pack a torch, a medical kit, gloves, windproof jacket and a survival blanket, both of their phones were in there too.

The trail opened out into a grassy area at the top of the hill with an electric pylon dominating the hilltop. Susan collapsed to the ground in its shadow, glad to finally be finished.

"Hey, you can't collapse just yet, we need a selfie. We have to commemorate your first ever trail run!" Jo said, digging the phones from the bag. She hauled Susan to her feet, "come on, there's an awesome view over here.

The view was indeed awesome, you could see for what seemed like miles from the other side of the hill, rolling countryside with the electrical lines running as straight as an arrow through the land. The furthest away pylon was so far you couldn't even tell there was one, just the vague notion of something holding up the powerline. Considering the looming mass of the one above their heads, Susan found this amazing. "Come on, get in here." Jo put her arm around her and angled the phone so that the view was visible over their left shoulders.

"I can't believe you put your arm around me, I'm so sweaty!" Susan said, actually starting to feel a little cold as the sweat dried.

"Hey, I'm showering when I get home anyway, doesn't matter how nasty I get now." She laid out the blanket over the long grass and started pulling ziplock bags out. "Geeze, are you feeding Africa or something? There's so much food here!"

Right enough, she had started with egg and cress sandwiches and added a pork pie, cold sausages, two Mars bars, crisps and dip and a big bottle of fizz. "Well, I wasn't sure how hungry we would be."

"Well, I'm not going past a pork pie. Want half?" Jo asked as she munched her half. "Oh, those are good!"

"Hey, I was thinking, you know how you eat lunch with those boys every second day?" Susan asked.

Jo's eyes narrowed, "Where's this going?"

"Well, I was thinking, perhaps I could hang out with all of you. You know, maybe once a week or something."

Jo's brows furrowed, "I didn't think you would want anything to do with them after what happened at the school gate. What brought this on?"

"Well, I thought with you getting to know all my friends it might be nice for me to know yours. You know, faces to names, perhaps if they get to know me they wouldn't resent me so much." Susan suggested.

"Hmmm," Jo searched her friend's face, seeing she was sincere she said, "I guess it can't hurt. As long as you realise most of them are immature idiots."

They ate their meal, chatting about school and life. Eventually, the conversation got around to university, Susan mentioned Heather's suggestion that they all share a flat.

"I think we would need a third couple before that would work." Jo said without thinking, she covered her mouth with her hand. "Oops, I mean two more couples." Then she realised that was wrong too and she cringed scrunching her eyes shut. "Damnit, I mean... we would need to be a couple and the others pair off?"

Susan laughed at her faux pas, "I know Abby and Anne are probably an item. Don't worry, it's our secret. And you know, I'm already getting called a lesbian at school so, I don't think it will matter too much coming out."

"I'm really sorry about that, hold on, is that you saying you will go out with me?" Jo asked, holding her breath.

"Depends, are you a good kisser?" Susan teased her.

Jo pulled her onto her lap, "why don't we find out?" She drew her into a passionate kiss that lasted what seemed like a lifetime to Susan. Her toes curled, fireworks went off in her brain and it seemed every nerve ending tingled.

"Whooie, I think that's a yes." Susan said with a satisfied sigh. "If I weren't such a sweaty mess I might have let you ravish me here and now!"

"I think perhaps we should take it a little slower than that, not that I don't want to but you know, propriety and such. I don't want to take advantage of the sweet innocent new lesbian!" Susan swatted her shoulder but then leaned in for another kiss, a softer, sweeter one this time.

"I guess we should head home. Want to help me break the news to my parents?" Susan asked.

Jo looked horrified. "Perhaps you don't have to come out. In fact, yes let's keep it secret and sneak about, that's fine!"

"Oh come on, you've done it once, how hard can it be?" Susan teased her.

"Well, when you're the big bad butch lesbian who's corrupted their sweet innocent daughter, I would say it could be pretty bad." Jo replied with a grimace.

"Hey, can we keep it a secret from Lucia's parents? Apparently, she's been told to stop hanging around with you because lesbians are the devil or some religious nonsense." Susan asked.

"Since when? I really don't want to get her in trouble! Perhaps I can stop hanging out with you guys at breaks?" Jo asked, shocked that she had caused Lucia problems.

"Nah, she doesn't care, her mum doesn't know who she's seeing at school. It was last weekend and you've hung out with her loads since then." Susan dismissed her concerns and finished packing the bag.

They headed off back down the trail, there were still a few upward bits but in general, Jo had been right, downhill rocked.

ele

"So, no parental units for the whole day." Abby said after shutting the door.

"Yep." Anne said with a smile, "but we do have Kelly."

Anne's parents were off to a baby shower for one of her colleagues and Abby's were playing golf. They had foolishly been left in charge of Anne's sister.

"So, want to get naked and have sex?" Abby joked, referring to her tragic attempt at flirtation the day Abby came out to her.

"Hell no, Kelly's here, I do not trust her not to barge in, intentionally." Anne said bitterly.

Abby looked at her questioningly, "she's not that bad."

"Tell that to someone who hasn't been asked to have words with her about ogling women in the shower!" Anne insisted.

"Oh, now this must be good." Abby dragged Anne to the sitting room, "explain, gory details please."

Anne explained what had happened, and her mortification at the woman's words.

"Honestly, I think she knew about both of us. I mean, eye contact. God, I almost died of embarrassment."

Abby laughed, "So how did the talk go?"

Anne rolled her eyes and stumped into the sofa, "What talk? I'm not about to explain locker room etiquette to my sister! Shit, turns out I don't even know locker room etiquette!"

"Can I do it? Please?"

"What, you want to give my sister a lecture?" She shook her head, "have at it!"

Abby didn't waste time, she called Kelly down from her room, "Sit young lady." She said pointing at the other end of the sofa. She paced back and forth with her hands behind her back, doing her best school-marm impression. "Now, it has come to our attention that in addition to being a handsy little girl, you also are a peeping tomboy!"

She turned to give Kelly a firm stare. "This. Must. Stop." She punctuated each word with a wave of her finger. "Now, as connoisseurs of the female form, we all know how hard it is not to look. We also know how ridiculous it appears when one so obviously averts their eyes, Anne!"

"Now, the correct protocol is to pay attention neck up, and I am speaking to both of you, sliding the eyes across someone's body should be a slide, quick and without meaning, simply moving your eyes from one focal point to another. One does not linger on their derriere when their backs are turned, Kelly, nor does one intently stare at the floor, Anne!" She resumed her pacing, "Now, if someone speaks, you make eye contact, and maintain eye contact." Both girls getting the lecture appeared to be trying to escape through the backs of their chairs.

"Now, there will be a practical test, our group visit to the pool is scheduled for two weeks today. Make note, I will be watching, and I assure you, someone is almost always, watching!"

"Any questions? No, well then, class dismissed!" Both Kelly and Anne took off towards their rooms at a run, faces beetroot. Abby put her pinky to her lip and gave her best Dr Evil laugh.

She caught up with Anne in her room, "Sorry, I couldn't help myself, you were both so cute, all embarrassed and red!"

Anne threw her pillow at her and laughed, "yeah, I guess it was quite funny."

"So, talking about inappropriate conduct, should we talk about a certain art student and her fantasies?" She smiled when she saw Abby's embarrassed look. "You know, if you need a life drawing model, I may be available." She was only teasing but on seeing Abby's face light up she blushed herself.

"Are you seriously willing? I mean, I could get my art stuff and be back in like, twenty minutes?" Anne's brain shut down on hearing this. Part of her wanted to say no, to run for the hills, unfortunately, the part of her in control of her face waggled her eyebrows suggestively.

Abby didn't need any more permission, she was out of the door and down the street before Anne's synapses fired again. 'oh shit, oh shit, oh shit, what have I just agreed to?' she thought. Her next thought, difficult though it was to hear over the hammering of her heart, was to look down the top of her t-shirt, 'need to change, need to change!' she frantically hunted through her underwear drawer, she knew she had a nice simple black bra and undies that kind of matched. The entire drawer was pulled out and tossed on the bed, "there you are!" She exclaimed under her breath. Tossing the remainder back in the drawer she wedged her chair under the door handle, she had no idea if that worked but you saw it on movies all the time. She got naked and then fully dressed again in what may just have been a world record time, her faded and worn old white bra and panties went in the laundry basket and after a second's thought were buried under yesterday's uniform.

She sat on the bed, heart still thumping and hands shaking, she bit her lip and remembered to pull the chair away. 'shitshitshit, this is a terrible idea!' She repeated to herself. She got up and went to brush her teeth, both because she foresaw lots of kissing and for something to occupy her. The minty taste calmed her down a little. She put on deodorant too, picking the most antiperspirant one they had, then after some thought took her shirt off and sprayed her entire torso.

She returned to her bedroom with the thought, 'Oh god why am I doing this?'

—— *ele* ——

"I'm just surprised it wasn't Lucia." Susan's mum smacked his arm, "well, you know, they were thick as thieves."

They were standing in Susan's conservatory, well, Jo and Susan were standing, her parents were calmly sitting on the couch. They had decided to sleep on the decision, then they had taken most of the day to work up the courage to actually tell Susan's parents. They had been bizarrely calm and accepting, as if they had expected this. Jo stood holding Susan's hand, searching the adult's faces for some hint of... anything. It had been like saying 'I like Chinese food' there was that little reaction.

"I'm happy for you honey, now, sit down, you two look so uncomfortable standing there." They sat, almost on autopilot. "Now Jo, would your mum be upset if I poured you a glass of wine to celebrate?"

"Oh, erm, no thanks, I'm in training so..." Jo stammered. "But don't let that stop Susan."

"Well, I have some non-alcoholic stuff in the cellar, back in a second." Jo looked at Susan who seemed as perplexed as she was.

"So, you're okay with me dating your daughter? You don't mind?" She asked Susan's father.

"Oh god no, it's a modern world, why would it matter?" He finished his wine and poured another. "Anyway, we can look on the bright side, no unexpected bundles of joy!"

"I didn't expect you to react this way. It's all a bit..." Jo started, "Confusing." Finished Susan.

"Here we go Jo, it's just Lindauer but apparently it's not bad, according to my gym buddies." She handed her a champagne flute of what looked like fizzy wine. She then filled another glass with still wine from the open bottle and handed it to her daughter.

"Well, I guess 'Welcome to the family!'" she held her glass out and they all obediently clinked glasses. "Wait till I tell them at the gym, exciting news. I love it!"

"So, what are your plans for my daughter?" her father asked leaning forwards, "Are you going to make an honest woman of her? How do you intend to support your new family?" Jo's face went from puzzled to wide-eyed bafflement, "Sorry, I always thought I would have to do the intimidation thing when she brought a boy home, figured this may be my only chance."

"Dad!" Susan complained, "Hold on! Was that a 'Susan's pregnant' pre-rehearsed speech?"

"It may have been. You know, it was one of my biggest fears!" He laughed.

Susan shook her head and put her arm around Jo's waist, "I was actually going to ask you. What do you think about me applying for the local Uni rather than going somewhere hundreds of miles away?"

Her mum almost spilt her drink in the rush to hug her, "I'm all for that! Oh, it would be so good to have you close."

"Well, I guess I would be the villain if I said anything else." her father said.

"Erm, I was wondering though, would it be possible to get a flat or something nearer the university?" she tentatively asked.

"Let me guess, and move in with your girlfriend? I'm not sure I trust you that much." his wife elbowed him in the ribs.

"I think it's a great idea honey." She looked at the girls, "that is as long as they can prove they can work hard for the rest of this year without letting their relationship get in the way?"

"Hmmm, I'm not convinced, there's a big difference when you're living together, no forced separation to do homework for one." He frowned, "we could just make you live in the halls of residence. If I recall correctly you can do that for two years of your course."

"Oh come on Rick, they're responsible, and you've eaten the food in those places!"

He grumbled but gave in, "Fine, but I want to see some really good grades this year. From both of you!"

The next day the newly minted couple walked hand in hand down the corridors to their group's usual corner, they drew a number of stares but had decided they could weather the snide comments and homophobic reactions.

What they didn't expect was tears from Lucia, she had taken one look at them and ran, tears flowing freely down her cheeks.

"Erm... what just happened?" Susan asked.

"She just got through telling us that her mother's church has all their kids spying on her. She was saying she had to avoid Jo in public places because she has no idea who is actually doing the spying." Heather explained.

"Oh, crap..." Susan closed her eyes, she couldn't believe how badly timed this was. "Why didn't she tell us on the bus?"

"Hey, you didn't tell us your news either." Jenny reminded her.

"Well, I wanted Jo to be here, god I feel bad. We already pretty much came out to the whole school just by holding hands. Shit, her mum's not going to let me see her ever again!" She slumped to the ground and put her face in her hands. Jo awkwardly rubbed her shoulder, unsure of what she could say to make this better.

"Well, I'm going to go find Lucia." Heather said, striding off.

"Tell her I'm sorry." Susan called after her.

"Apparently she's grounded for two months!" Anne said, "and banned from movie night forever."

"What? But that's our thing! Oh god, how did I fuck this up so badly." Susan buried her head in her arms. "And it's the man who fell to earth this week." She mumbled to herself, "She always watches that film with me."

"Well, congratulations on your new relationship. I'm happy for you and all that jazz but I'm going to go find Lucia too." Jenny said with a wave.

"And suddenly the lesbians are on their own." Jo said quietly.

There was a shocked intake of breath for Anne, "Oh, yeah, Susan figured it out. Don't worry, it's between us."

"Really?" She asked, looking at Susan for confirmation, "Even so, don't say things like that at school." Anne said, looking around furtively. "Someone might hear. Not to be insensitive, but I still want to be able to hang out with Lucia."

"It's weird, people seem to have stopped accusing me of being a lesbian since Susan came out." Anne said, currently lying in Abby's bed with her head resting on Abby's shoulder, they were both reading the same book which turned out to be logistically difficult. "I'm done."

Abby flicked the page, "I feel sorry for Susan, have you heard the names she's been called?"

"I think she quite likes Sapphic Sue!" Anne chuckled, "at least she can be openly affectionate at school now."

"Yeah, but she effectively lost her best friend for that benefit."

"Makes me feel doubly bad thinking we may not be able to hang out with her if we come out."

"I'm done." Abby flicked the next page, "It's a bummer she can't come for movie night tomorrow, I think it's the first one she's ever missed."

"Pretty sure it is, it's going to be weird without her." Abby agreed.

"I'm done." Anne said, "You know, Susan said telling her parents was really easy, they're super supportive and accepting."

"Yeah, but if we told our parents do you think we would get to do this?" She put her book down and slipped her hand across onto Anne's stomach then kissed the top of her head. "Anyway, homework is done. What now?"

"I'm tempted to read the rest of the book, I like this." Anne suggested.

"I like it too but I've already read the whole book so I'm less keen!" Abby admitted, "Want to see my painting? It's coming along really nicely."

She disentangled herself from Anne and fetched a canvas from under her bed. "It's got some work needed. I'm not happy with the hand

and I'm still to finish the background but I think it's rather good."

Anne blushed, "It is good, really good. I'm glad I didn't let you talk me into taking my bra off, this thing is going to hang on our wall at some point. I don't want our guests seeing me naked!"

"Ooooh, already fantasizing about living with me? I'm flattered." She put the painting back under the bed. "You know, I could do a tasteful one that doesn't show anything? Something like you sitting looking back over your shoulder, the bare expanse of your back, a hint of bum?"

"Finish this one and we'll see." Anne said firmly. Once she had gotten over her initial shyness she had actually enjoyed modelling for her girlfriend, Abby had obviously appreciated it and her picture was nice, though she thought it was perhaps overly flattering. "At least this one is big enough that I know you won't carry it to school!"

"Erm, yeah, about that. I need a portfolio for university applications, I was wondering if perhaps you would let me... use this one?" Anne's eyes widened at the request. "And no one at school would see it, and you're not naked in it!" The eyes narrowed, "or perhaps you could model for a different one? Fully clothed?" Abby fumbled with her bedspread. "It's just, I really like this one."

"Tell you what, I will promise to model for you for a few more and if that one is still needed, well, we can talk about it." Anne relented. She chewed her lip for a while, "and I might just let you do the back one."

Abby tackled Anne into a hug, "thankyouthankyouthankyou!" She squealed, bouncing with excitement. "Can we do a clothed one now? I can do a really quick charcoal?"

Not wanting to disappoint her, Anne submitted to modelling for another hour until Abby's parents got home.

The mood at Anne's house on Saturday was far more sombre, the fact that Lucia wasn't coming was at the forefront of their minds. It wasn't helped when Pete asked "Susan, where's your partner in crime?"

"She was banned from coming to any more movie nights." Susan confessed, "because her mum doesn't like her associating with gay people."

"What! In this day and age?" Pete asked astounded that people could be so closed-minded.

"It's a religious thing." She explained, shaking her head.

"So, you didn't suggest that perhaps Jo sits this one out, perhaps alternate months?" Pete suggested, "It seems like a pretty knee jerk reaction."

"It didn't help that she lied and saw Jo at school, apparently their mosque has all their children spying on her."

"Well, I can see that looks bad, so now she's having to avoid Jo at school too?" He asked, feeling bad for the girl.

"And me." Susan said quietly, averting her eyes.

"She's avoiding you? But you guys have been inseparable since the beginning of high school!" He frowned, "what happened?"

She met his eyes again and squeezed out, "I'm Jo's girlfriend."

Pete could see she was close to tears, "Oh no, come here!" He said and gathered her in a hug. "It's not your fault, you can't help who you're attracted to." He rubbed her back, "There, there, at least she still has Anne and the girls, I'm glad they don't have to deal with this bigotry." This just caused Susan to cry more and left him wondering what he had said wrong.

They ate their pizza and didn't linger for long downstairs, even the film was quiet, the choice hadn't helped.

"I'm not sure having Bowie in it helped..." Heather mused.

"It was, erm, pretty weird." Agreed Jenny, "is that what they mean when they say it's an 'arthouse' film?"

"I quite liked it, it was thought-provoking. It's all about people's fear of the unknown and the removal of personal liberties. The filmography was a little distracting though." Jo felt she needed to defend the movie for Susan's sake but she did genuinely like it.

"Thanks, Jo, I think perhaps it was just the wrong day for it. And I can admit, it looks like it bored Kelly to tears!" Susan said, accepting the film hadn't gone down well. "How about we watch another Bowie classic?" She held up another DVD, "Labyrinth!"

There were cheers of acceptance. "You know, apparently there's a drinking game people do whilst watching this? You drink every time you see Bowie's ... package, as it were." Jenny explained, "I think we should do that, cheer and take a slug of our drinks, it's symbolic!"

"You didn't spike the punch did you Jenny?" Anne joked.

"What punch?" Jenny asked, not getting the joke.

"Never mind, just put the film on, let's do this!" Anne raised her glass, "charge your glasses girls!"

Labyrinth cheered them up, it was a fun film and the faux drinking game made it even more entertaining. Had they been drinking spirits they would all have been hammered by the end of the movie.

It was still relatively early when the films finished so Jo led them in a singalong, just a few songs but it was fun, even Mae joined in.

When Susan drew the next film it was Jo again, "I ring the bullshit bell, it's rigged!" Susan called.

"What do you mean? It was your choice this week!" Anne asked her.

"Oh, shit, we never did tell you, did we? Jo cheated for me and put my choice on her paper too." She looked suitably embarrassed.

"So that film was Jo's fault! I think it's a redraw, Susan can't draw if it wasn't her film!" Abby insisted. The film went back in the bag and Jo drew the next film.

"Okay, sorry guys, it must be rigged! Next month's movie is 'Rain Man'. That was my choice." She handed Anne the paper to prove it.

There were choruses of "Redraw!" But Anne spoke up in her best courtroom voice, "There's no rule against drawing your own film, the selection stands! The bag knows, the bag picks!"

Once the "awws" had died down she continued "Before we split up and do our teeth, it's my birthday this week. I was wondering if people might like to come ice-skating with me next Saturday and we can swim another time?"

"I forgot Anne was the baby of the group! She always acts so mature." Heather teased, "holy cow, you're going to be stuck at home for months after we're old enough to go to the pub!"

"Good point, I must be seven months older than you! Geez, who'd have thought?" Jo said in amazement.

"It's just because I'm so much smarter than you all!" Anne defended herself, they went through this almost every year.

"So, are you staying on for a sixth year?" Mae asked in her quiet voice.

This was a new one for Anne, normally they just teased her, "I wasn't planning it, I think everyone else is applying for uni this year. No way I'm letting these idiots get ahead of me, they might start forgetting how smart I am!"

"So, you're applying before Christmas and hoping for conditional acceptance?" Mae continued, this was obviously a topic she was interested in.

"Well, yeah, my grades are good so I don't expect to fail anything. And I'm planning on applying for something science-related, possibly applied chemistry or materials science. I mean, I'm pretty much top of the class in all the sciences and maths." She glanced at Susan, "And there was a suggestion we should all apply for the local university, if so the entrance requirements are lower than some of the places I was looking at."

"Are you talking about Heather's dream of a shared flat like in friends?" Jenny asked.

"It does sound nice, perhaps two flats like they had, across the hall." Anne said wistfully.

Mae fidgeted with her pyjama buttons for a second, "Could I join in? Get a nearby flat? All my friends at school are going all over the place, one is even going to study in Canada. I was thinking I could wait a year and see where everyone got accepted so I could follow someone but then I would be in the wrong year, and hardly any of my friends are doing a sixth year."

"Hey, at the moment we haven't decided but if you don't mind being close to home, sure. We'll need to get our parents on board though." Anne assured her.

"Hey, speak for yourself! It's that or nothing for me, I'm relying on handouts to be able to afford even that." Jo piped up. "I don't know how the scholarship works, whether I would get an accommodations allowance or if I need to commute from home but I would like to live near all you guys."

"So, how's the application going?" Heather asked, "anything you need help with."

"Nope, Jenny's mum helped me and it's already been collected and submitted. She seemed really upset I wasn't into those lgbgt rallies and gay rights shenanigans but you know, I'm just not into that stuff. Being a gay teenager is hard enough without having to protest all the time."

"Pretty sure that's a car Jo." Abby sniggered.

"You're thinking mgbgt, but I don't think it's right either." Heather corrected her.

"Well, the alphabet soup crowd. I don't know, lesbian is enough of a stigmatic label for me."

"Hey, you sidetracked my birthday arrangements!" Anne exclaimed just having realised no one had said they were coming.

"Yeah, we'll all be there." Heather said dismissively, "so, how's this flat thing going to work? How do we find multiple flats in the same building? Do we get our parents to buy them as an investment or just rent?"

The next morning Anne woke to find she and Abby were the last up, the others must have all been very quiet speaking out as neither of the girls had woken. She was mortified to find she was snuggled up against Abby. "Do you think they noticed?" She asked once she had woken her girlfriend.

"You mean one of the three who don't already know? At the moment I'm thinking it might be easiest to tell them." Abby said with a yawn. "They've been pretty accepting of Susan."

Anne got a slightly panicked look in her eyes, "I don't think I'm ready, maybe after Christmas?"

Abby thought back to Jo's story about her last girlfriend. "Yeah, we can wait. We're all alone just now though..." she leaned in for a kiss.

After breaking apart Anne panted, "They could come up at any time though."

"Better be quick then!" Abby kissed her again, this time slipping her hand under her top and across the smooth skin of her back.

Anne gave a little, "Hmmm" and committed fully to the kiss, Abby's hands wandered, slipping down to cup her bum causing Anne to tense up.

'Damn!' Abby thought and moved her hand back to safer locations. Once she did she was pleased to feel the warmth of Anne's hand on her back, skin on skin.

Too soon Anne broke off the kiss, "come on, I can smell bacon." She said, dragging her girlfriend to her feet.

When they got to the kitchen Jo gave them a knowing look, "I was just about to come to get you two lazybones. We've been up long enough to do the crosswords."

"Normal and cryptic!" Kelly called out, as if she had done the bulk of the work.

They sat at the breakfast bar, Pete and Jane vacated their seats having finished breakfast ages ago. Anne poured them both muesli and ladled honey flavoured yoghurt on top.

"The girls all seem to be looking forward to ice-skating with you Anne, have you set a time?" Jane asked, mainly because she knew she hadn't.

"I have to phone the rink, make sure there isn't any large booking I need to avoid." Anne replied after she finished chewing her mouthful of cereal, "But I was thinking we could grab a burger and skate after if the evening is free?"

"Evenings on Saturday is ice dancing, they put on music and disco lights." Mae said, then when everyone gave her a surprised look she quietly said, "I quite like skating."

"Erm, Mae, do they allow newbies on during ice dancing? Cos' I've never skated in my life. I mean, I'm keen, I want to try but... " Jo asked, not wanting to spoil people's fun.

"Yeah, they don't care. There are fewer little kids there too so it's probably a better time to learn."

"And I can hold your hands." Susan said with a smile.

CONFRONTATION

It was a beautiful late autumn day and everyone had agreed to meet outside for lunch. They liked to meet in the courtyard formed by the cafeteria, the science classrooms and the maths block. It had a corner of two low retaining walls to sit on and a tree to lean against.

So far only Abby and Jo had arrived, the others were probably still queuing in the cafeteria.

"Nothing against Anne, I love her to bits but I'm kind of glad you were her fantasy when she got herself off. It sounds like she's really against coming out. Not only that but Susans just so..." Jo couldn't think of how to finish that sentence, Susan was so many things, nice, smart, generous, fun, understanding, a great kisser, hot as hell. "... perfect."

Abby laughed, "you know she didn't? I'm not saying it was bad advice, and it did get us together in a way but... she still hasn't." She squirmed uncomfortably on the broad wooden fence.

"What? Oh my god!" Jo's eyes went wide. "So, you guys haven't made it to fourth base then?"

"If I understand the whole base thing, I haven't made it to second base! And stupidly I said to myself that I was swearing off... you know... till erm, Anne did. God, I'm frustrated. I just want to pin her down and... well you know." Abby trailed off, embarrassed. "How about you and Susan?"

"Yeah, second, I'm taking it slowly, don't want to rush her." Jo said with a slight blush.

"I really don't want to scare Anne off by pushing her too far, after that fiasco the first night. Urg." Abby shook her head.

"I never did hear that story." Jo pushed.

"And you won't, not from me. Shh." She said, seeing the others coming over with their lunch.

On the way back to class Susan was shoulder barged, she took a tumble down half a flight of steps. She lay for a second, dazed and in pain. "You should watch where you're going, dyke." Spat the girl who had shoved her. It was one of the popular girls who always had a gaggle of friends hanging onto every word, "Perhaps if you weren't checking out the girls in front of you, you would have seen where you were walking."

Suddenly a male voice said, "Fuck off Tanya," a bulky body interposed itself between Susan and the girl. "It was obvious you did that on purpose." He took a step forward, forcing the girl to take a step back and stumble over the bottom stair, falling on her arse.

"Perhaps if you feel so threatened by someone else's choice of partner you should take a long hard look at yourself, maybe you're compensating for something? Or perhaps you're jealous? Doesn't feel so nice does it, someone casting those same aspersions back at you!" He looked around at the speechless hangers-on shaking his head.

Looking back at Tanya he continued, "Someone else's gender preferences don't mean they lust after every member of that sex. Take me for example, I'm firmly hetero but I am actually repulsed by you, and it's nothing to do with what's under your clothes, it's what's inside that makes you so vile."

He held out his hand to Susan and helped her to her feet, "Did she hurt you?" He asked, still supporting her arm as they walked away.

"No, just bruised." She admitted.

"Good, let me walk you to class." As he said that Heather joined them.

They walked away, leaving the girl on the ground surrounded by her posse "I heard what you said, aren't you the one that accosted Susan at the gate the other week?" He nodded self-consciously, "why the big change of heart?"

"Well, Jo knocked some sense into me, literally. Also, Susan has been hanging out with us at lunch, I can see why Jo likes her." Susan blushed a little at this.

"So, want to come ice skating this weekend?" Heather impulsively asked him.

"Heather, you can't just ask someone to someone else's birthday party!" Susan exclaimed.

"Sure I can, he can be my dance partner! So, what do you say?" The poor boy looked like a rabbit caught in the headlights. "I'll take that as a yes, it's starting at six in the burger place next door."

"Erm...okay?" The boy managed.

They got to their maths class and sat down, all three a little shocked after the event, though perhaps for different reasons.

"So, Heather and Brian eh? I guess I was wrong about at least one of Anne's friends!" Jo quipped, jogging easily along the trail with Susan puffing at her side.

They had been running once or twice a week since that first date and Susan had been training on the roads alone. She could now manage multiple kilometres without collapsing with her lungs on fire. That didn't mean she could keep up with Jo though, the ease she loped along beside her was amazing, Susan couldn't help feeling proud of her girlfriend.

"He's actually quite a nice guy when he hasn't worked himself up about something." Susan said, in between panted breaths.

"Yeah, and he tells me he hasn't smoked a cigarette in a week." Jo said in amazement.

"Well, you stopped ages ago, you never suggested you found it hard." Susan was close to stopping, the 'conversational pace' that Jo had set was a little fast for talk in her mind.

"Yeah, I was used to cold turkey weekends and evenings though. It's a bit harder now that I'm trying to stop the patches though."

Susan waved her down and they slowed to a walk. "I don't know how you smoked and ran, I've never had a cigarette in my life and my lungs are fit to burst."

They stopped for a minute to admire the evening view, over in the distance rain was obscuring the countryside.

"I'm faster now I think, so yeah it probably was holding me back." She was looking at the way the clouds were moving. "Might be best to turn back rather than do the circuit, I think the weatherman got it wrong."

They double-timed it down the hill, the feeling of the wind rushing past and banking into the corners was exhilarating, unlike the first time she had run, Susan pushed herself on the downhill, gravity helping but not doing all the work this time. The gravel crunched rhythmically under their feet and all thought of conversation was forgotten. Susan felt that no matter how she pushed, Jo could have run double her speed, the way she ran seemed effortless.

In the end, they didn't make it back before the downpour, the sheets of ice-cold rain were refreshing though, cooling the tired muscles and helping with the last push back out of the countryside and down the streets towards Jo's house.

When they arrived soaked and dripping into the house Jo's mum ushered them straight into the bathroom, "You girls have a shower and dry off, don't drip all over my carpets. On you go loves."

Susan was shocked, it seemed to her they were being told by Jo's mother to strip and shower... together. She looked at Jo as the door shut and saw her embarrassed flush, emboldened by this she smiled and stripped off her top. She took in Jo's attempts not to look and stepped forward, she took hold of the bottom of Jo's shirt and gave her a questioning glance. Seeing acceptance she lifted the shirt up over Jo's head.

She bit her lip as the tight muscle of Jo's chest was revealed and reached behind herself, unclipping her sports bra and letting it fall to the floor. Jo's gaze lingered on Susan's body as she reached up and self consciously peeled off the nipple protectors from her own chest.

They were about to kiss when there was a bang on the door, "and no hanky panky!" Jo's mum shouted, seemingly as an afterthought. The girls giggled and Jo tore her gaze away long enough to turn on the shower.

Susan picked up both their shirts and wrung them out in the sink then turned to see Jo hesitantly shrug out of her long shorts. Every inch of her body was muscled, Susan stepped out of her own shorts and into the shower, pulling Jo in behind her.

The hot water was a relief, the cold had become intense since they stopped running and her feet tingled like pins and needles in the hot water.

She kissed Jo, long and lingering and her hands wandered over her body. Before they could get far however there was another banging on the door. "You hear me girls?" Jo broke the kiss and called "yes mum!" Before looking apologetically to Susan, she bit her lip and said, "soap my back?"

There wasn't much hanky panky in the shower but also, there wasn't none.

The girls skated in circles, the rink wasn't too busy but there were a lot of very accomplished skaters there. Amazingly Mae was one of them, she moved rhythmically to the thumping beat, spinning and jumping in time, Heather was almost as good but she was sticking close to Brian. Although the boy could skate, he wasn't good enough to dance like Mae was doing and Heather wasn't leaving him on his own much.

Jo was struggling, each of her friends were taking turns holding her hands and guiding her around the rink, normally one person holding each hand. Susan was right, she was pretty good, good enough to slowly skate backwards holding Jo's hands whenever it was her turn. Jo had insisted she not waste the whole night babysitting her and was enjoying watching her girlfriend dancing and turning on the ice.

"You two are amazing," Anne said when it was her turn to help Jo, "You both look so happy together."

"I think if you weren't trying to keep it secret you two would look just as happy." Jo suggested in a low voice, "make sure you dance with her tonight, no one will notice, see, everyone is dancing and holding hands with other girls."

Anne looked around and right enough, all the girls were dancing with each other. "Thanks," she said sincerely, "I'll do that as soon as someone takes over."

"Hey, I think I'm good enough now to go one lap of the rink on my own, go." She gave Anne a little shove, wobbling about precariously in the process.

Anne looked at her and, seeing she was skating okay, nodded, gliding off across the cold ice to find Abby. Jo spotted her girlfriend dancing with Mae, the two were doing moves she couldn't dream of, she couldn't imagine anyone being that comfortable on the slippery ice.

As she was watching she got distracted and didn't notice someone come twirling in from her left, they collided and Jo sailed across the ice on her stomach. People gave her and the other casualty a wide berth, trusting them to sort themselves out.

The girl who had collided with her got to her feet and said "oops" in a sarcastic tone of voice then skated away, leaving Jo fumbling about trying to regain her feet.

Kelly came over and helped her up, "You okay?" She asked, making sure she was steady on her feet.

"I don't think that was an accident." She said and as she did Susan skidded across the ice on her bum at the other side of the rink. "I think we're being targeted."

She hadn't recognised the girl who knocked her over, she probably couldn't even pick her out of the other dancers on the ice. "Let's go see if Susans is okay."

Susan and Mae had stopped dancing and were holding the side of the rink, "did you see that? She came out of nowhere." Susan asked as they joined them.

"I only caught the aftermath, Kelly was helping me up from my own collision. I don't know if I'm being paranoid but she didn't sound sorry."

As they were talking they saw Anne take a tumble on the ice, taking about four other skaters down with her. "That can't be a coincidence!" They made their way over to Anne and Abby.

"Did you see who did it?" Jo asked once they had all gathered around.

"No, I just got bumped as I was overextended, why?"

"Jo thinks people are intentionally knocking us down. It is a bit odd, three of us in a row." As she said that their last two friends arrived, looking a little flushed.

"This is good fun, pretty tiring though." Brian said, still holding Heather's hand.

"We're just trying to work out whether people were intentionally knocking us down." They were looking at the faces of the people whizzing past, trying to identify anyone they knew.

"I don't recognise anyone, are you sure it wasn't a coincidence?" Heather asked.

"No, not for certain but perhaps we should stick together in larger groups for a bit."

They split into two groups of four and nothing happened for a number of laps, the friends being very diligent in looking out for each other. When they eventually broke apart almost instantly Susan went sailing on her stomach.

"I saw that, someone pushed her but I lost her in the crowd." Brian said as they were helping Susan up.

"I'm done. I'm going to talk to the management." Jo declared, their group moved off the ice and clumsily made their way to the booth where they had gotten their skates.

"Hi, do you guys have a recording of what happens on the ice? My friends and I are being harassed by someone."

The spotty teenager behind the counter grunted and said something unintelligible into his walkie talkie.

When the manager eventually arrived he was a mountain of a man, imposing in height, stature and girth. Surprisingly though, he was very understanding when the girls explained the issue.

He spent about twenty minutes looking through the footage on camera before he returned, USB stick in hand.

"Well, it's not completely clean cut from the footage but it certainly looks like there may be one girl deliberately tripping you up." He handed the stick to Jo, "You don't see her face and the quality is pretty bad so I doubt it's enough to make it a police matter but perhaps you can take it to the school, just bring me back the stick when you're done."

"Just now though, how about I come out on the ice and watch to see if I can spot something happening? If so I can drag them off the ice and chuck them out for you."

The girls discussed this and decided taking it to the principal may be better than involving the police in what they would likely see as a schoolyard dispute.

The big man made his way onto the ice, he skated a few leisurely laps of the rink before Susan and Mae casually returned. They had decided as a group that there was no need for them all to return and the rest surreptitiously watched from a safe distance.

After a few slow twirls around the ice, the two experienced skaters started to do more adventurous moves, it almost looked like rock and roll dancing. They were really getting into it when a girl in a white jacket and scarf over her mouth rocketed in, the girls had obviously been paying attention however and they split apart at the last moment causing their assailant to fly straight into the side of the rink having expected to pass most of her momentum to Susan and Mae.

Within seconds the manager had swooped in and accosted the girl, as he dragged her bodily off the ice the scarf came down and it became obvious it was indeed Tanya.

"I bet she heard me invite Brian, we were just up the stairs weren't we?" Heather asked.

"Yeah, her or one of her cronies." Brian agreed. "I guess we can get back on the ice now, crisis averted!"

They didn't wait to see what happened to the girl, instead returning to the rink and making sure to have a good time.

Once they were all thoroughly cold and tired they went to return their boots. In the backroom, they could see Tanya sitting in a chair, the towering manager behind his desk watching her.

"What's happening?" Anne asked the spotty boy behind the counter.

"He called her parents, they're going to collect her. I think he's banning her from the rink too." The boy croaked, sounding like his voice was in the process of breaking.

"Cool, can you possibly thank the manager for me? I don't want to go in there just now but we appreciate everything he did."

"Sure." The boy nodded, taking the skates and spraying disinfectant into them.

Anne agonised over the incident for the rest of the weekend, realising that though Tanya had been caught and possibly punished by her parents for the bullying outside of school, it didn't mean she wouldn't retaliate during school.

The girl had proven her willingness to hurt her friends already, multiple times.

She eventually asked her father for advice and showed him the footage from the ice rink.

"Well, the manager is right, you can tell it's the same girl but only just and you never see her face. As proof goes, it's not ironclad." He thought for a few minutes, holding his chin and tapping his cheek with his index finger.

He held up his finger, "Wait here." He instructed her and strode off into the garage. When he returned he was holding his dashcam and Anne's bag.

"You carry this around all day don't you?" Anne nodded. "Okay, do you still have that USB power bank we got you for Christmas?" Again she nodded. "Right, go get it, I'll nip and get my tools."

When she came back her dad had cut a small hole in the outside layer of her bag, through into the front pocket. "Right, pass me the battery. Is it charged?" He asked.

"Yeah, I just unplugged it." She answered.

He took out a roll of foam tape marked UHB and carefully cut strips to go round the camera lens and down the flat body then he pressed the other side onto the inside of the pocket, making sure the lens was visible through the small hole.

"Right, just the cable up through here and pop the power bank into this little internal pocket. There, one spy bag, ready to go. Shall we test it?" He asked with a smile.

He plugged in the power. Nothing visibly happened as the little red light that normally came on was hidden by the tape, he put the bag on her back and she walked around. "Okay, simulating me pushing you." He walked up behind her and gave a gentle shove. "Great, let's get the sd card and check if that was okay."

They plugged the card into his laptop and right enough, in glorious HD goodness was everything from the viewpoint of the bag, including a perfect image of his face as he pushed her even better it even captured audio.

"Right, no taking this into the locker rooms or toilets! That may get you and me in trouble." He reinserted the card and set her bag on the table. "Now, that covers you for a rear attack, I would suggest for breaks and lunch you find a wall or a corner and point the bag away from you. You okay with that?"

Anne nodded, quite relieved that she would have some proof if something happened.

"Now, tomorrow morning when the office opens I'm going to call up and explain what happened, I will make sure they know to keep an eye out but I will tell them not to make a fuss unless something actually happens. That way at least they will have been pre-warned and will be more likely to take your side." He gave her a little hug, "And try to keep together. There's strength in numbers okay?"

Anne was nervous, her dad had told her not to mention the camera to her friends and now she felt it as a pressure, weighing down on her, lies by omission. She felt that every response she made, every comment was a falsehood, her interactions felt stilted, delayed and considered as if she were editing her lines on the fly. She hated it.

The bus ride seemed to drag, she found herself focusing on the diesel smell, the rough feeling of the coarse tartan material under her thighs and fingertips, the whine of the gearbox, anything to distract her from the conversation which felt like a betrayal of her friends.

By the time the bus came rumbling into the school car park she had decided to tell her friends, just not at school, she was going to stick it out for the day and tell them on the way home. This gave her some relief, a loosening of the guilt she felt.

They stuck together, by common consensus rather than any instruction from Anne, even so, there didn't seem to be a need. There was no sign of Tanya, not before class as they hung out with Jo in the cafeteria nor during any of the breaks, it seemed she may have been actively avoiding them. That suited them to a tee and by the time she got off the bus with Abby, Anne had forgotten the camera entirely. To the point that she didn't tell anyone and didn't turn it off.

"So, my parents aren't home, you up for 'homework'?" Abby made the inverted commas with her fingers.

Anne gave her a sly look, "Modelling? I did wear the birthday present you got me." She couldn't believe how casual she had gotten with the idea of modelling almost naked in front of her girlfriend.

"Nice, I hope it wasn't too obvious that I really bought them for my own enjoyment?" They raced back to Abby's place, keen for some alone time.

They didn't even get to her room before their lips were locked together, climbing the stairs backwards, Anne fumbled with her buttons. When she got to the room she pulled her blouse off and Abby broke away, "I love the colour, purple suits you so well." She bit her lip, "going to show me the rest?"

"I don't know, I'm thinking tit for tat, perhaps I want you to undress and give me something to look at whilst you draw me?" She said cheekily, Abby didn't have to be asked twice and to Anne's shock she quickly stripped her uniform off, not stopping at her undies.

Anne sucked in a breath, her eyes opening wide in shock. Suddenly her teasing seemed to have gone too far. For the first time since they started dating her girlfriend was standing before her, naked as the day she was born. She let out a little "Hrm!" Biting her lip.

"Like what you see?" Abby asked, Anne could only nod, speechless.

Abby got her art supplies and an easel out, acting as if it were perfectly normal to be naked whilst drawing a life model. Anne could not tear her eyes from her nude form, for the first time in her life feeling like she didn't need to avert her eyes or not look directly, her girlfriend was gorgeous.

"Okay, I need you in a different pose, I was thinking if you scoot to the headboard and bring your knees up to your chest." It took a moment before Anne's brain processed this request and when she realised she had been staring, not responding for a few seconds she jumped to comply.

"Perfect, now, hug them to your chest. Perfect" Abby hurriedly did a pencil sketch, her hand flying over the taught canvas. "Hold on, I'll put on some music so you're not too bored."

She fiddled with her phone and a Bluetooth speaker, soon California Dreamin' was playing and Abby was back at the easel. Anne wondered why she thought she might get bored, just following Abby's naked body as she drew, engrossed in the hobby she obviously loved, was enthralling.

Before Anne knew it Abby was mixing up oil paint on an old wooden palette, she started slapping great swaths of dark paint on the canvas, working mainly with a palette knife. Once she was satisfied she mixed up some other colours, more flesh-toned paint than Anne had ever thought she would be comfortable with, again this was applied with gusto.

By the time Abby was finished roughing out the figure her playlist had stopped, neither girl noticed. Abby switched to finer brushes and her palate became full of shades, pinks and purples with some blue alongside, Anne was engrossed in the paint which didn't make it to the canvas, instead painting her girlfriend's body, small splashes of colour highlighting her thighs and breasts, coating her arms.

Suddenly there was a noise of the front door opening. Both Abby and Anne froze then, as they heard steps coming up the stairs darted into motion, finding and donning their discarded uniforms in a flash, uncaring of the paint which must have coated the interior of Abby's blouse.

They were presentable, barely, when Abby's mum opened the bedroom door without knocking. "Hey girls, I'm home." She said in a tired voice, "Anne, it's probably time for you to go home, it's almost dinner time." She hadn't noticed anything amiss and closed the door after her announcement.

Both girls let out a breath then devolved into fits of quiet giggles. Once she recovered, Anne quietly put her tights and shoes back on and tidied her clothing. She looked up to see Abby again topless and using a rag to wipe oil paint from her arms, she bit her lip and boldly walked over to her girlfriend to catch her lips in a kiss and run her fingers down Abby's bare side making absolutely certain she didn't get paint on her uniform. Abby was stuck, frustrated and unable to return the caress due to her paint-covered hands, "Finish it at the same time next week?" Anne whispered in her ear before turning and walking out.

ele

She got home, and her dad was the first to greet her, "How did it go? Do we need to get any footage off the camera?"

Amazed at herself, she realised she hadn't stopped the camera, it had been in the corner of the room the whole time. "No, we didn't see her all day." She quickly replied before racing off to her bedroom.

"Dinner will be ready in five!" Her dad called after her.

Getting to her room she turned on her computer, impatiently waiting for it to boot she pulled off her uniform and changed into jogging bottoms and a t-shirt. As soon as the machine had finished its boot process she inserted the USB cable from the camera which was still in her bag. The bing-bong tone telling her it was connected was accompanied by the window opening and showing the contents of the drive.

She quickly highlighted all the files and was about to press delete when she thought again. She cut the files and pasted them into her documents folder. Waiting impatiently for them to move.

"Girls! Dinner!" She heard her mum shout, seconds before the process completed. She pulled the cable and removed the battery from her bag, putting it on charge.

"Coming!" She called, itching to stay and see what the camera had been looking at.

—ell—

"Have you heard back from that application yet Joanne?" Her dad asked, for once he wasn't on night shift or backshift so he was eating dinner with them, all three sat around the small kitchen table.

"I won't hear until after Christmas, the others at school haven't even submitted their applications yet." She explained.

"So why did you do it so early?" He asked.

"Well, they're all really well off, I'm applying for a scholarship, I guess they need more time to get everything checked out." Jo guessed.

"It's all just checking how good your grades are and stuff though, surely it's no harder?"

"Well, I guess there are fewer places so they need to be more discerning?" She shrugged.

"So, there must be loads of people applying. Any idea how many places there are? How likely are you to get in?" Her mum asked.

"Well, Jenny's mum reckons I'm a shoo-in, as long as I keep my grades up. She says her recommendation counts a lot. Also, people can only apply if they can't afford the tuition fees so that limits the competition." Susan explained.

"How could they possibly know that?" Her dad asked, frowning.

Jo didn't notice the subtle shake of her mum's head and bulldozed straight in, "well, that's why they need your tax returns."

Her dad's face turned red, "Well there bloody well not getting them! You can tell those nosy buggers to keep their eyes to themselves, they're not allowed to poke into my business!"

"Now George, this is her future we're talking about, it's not like they're doing anything but checking they give money to the right people."

"No, I said no and I mean it, you're not giving my financial details to some organisation. Next I know, we'll be on some welfare list and they'll be sending social workers and busybodies to check up on us. I'm not having it and that's it." He threw his fork down and stormed out of the flat.

"What just happened?" Jo asked in a panic.

"Don't you worry, it's done and gone and we won't bring it up again. He's always been weird with money, that's why I may not have asked permission that day." Her mum patted her hand, "it's submitted now so there's nothing he can do."

"But mum... we need to prove each year that our circumstances haven't changed."

Physical

The next morning was wet, very wet. Anne and Abby were standing shivering at the uncovered bus stop huddling under a single umbrella, both wishing their uniforms included stout boots and trousers.

"So... we may have inadvertently made porn yesterday?" Abby whispered for the fourth time.

"Yes!, Stop saying it!" Anne hissed.

"And your bag is a camera?"

"Yes! Stop asking this over and over!"

"I think my brain melted." Abby said in a flat emotionless voice. "Can I watch it?"

"It's just you, standing and painting for hours." Anne insisted.

"Do I look hot? I've heard the camera adds ten pounds. How much is a pound?" She said, still seeming in a daze. "Hold on, you watched it. Did I look hot?"

"Abby, shut up! Yes, you looked hot okay! Just, shush! The bus will be here soon."

"Hot enough to get your motor running? Did I erm, hit the right buttons?" Abby asked, slightly more animatedly.

"No! Now shush, the bus is here."

Abby looked slightly disappointed but then instantly brightened up, "So I could still be there for your first time?" She said with a wicked smile which earned her a smack on the arm as the bus pulled up.

—*ele*—

Lucia had to get the second bus, none of her friends got the second bus but that was the point. Damn her mother.

She sat in silence whilst the wet streets slid past, at least on the second bus it wasn't likely people would need to sit beside her. Her mother had forced her to start wearing a headscarf. Ridiculous religious nonsense. She expected there may be an insistence to join the mosque soon. God, she hated that woman.

As a devout atheist she despised all religions, she wondered for the millionth time if she could claim asylum somewhere on religious grounds, or rather anti-religious. Salman Rushdie had done it hadn't he?

The rain was really bouncing off the road. She normally liked a good rainstorm, especially if there was thunder, today, however, it just added to her dreary outlook.

Her friends had tried, they really had, they took shifts being with her at breaks and having lunch with her. It wasn't the same, the grounding meant she couldn't go to their coffee shop, or bowling or anything fun. School, homework, bed, rinse, repeat. It was dull.

She sighed as the bus pulled into the school, another day. She told herself it was another day closer to her eighteenth birthday and freedom. She was having horrific thoughts however that perhaps she may not get to go to university. Her mother seemed to be enjoying her stranglehold if she convinced her father not to fund her university education. Ugh.

She traipsed slowly up the stairs, her registration class was on the top floor of the maths department. The last bus was still fairly early and so she had nothing to do for a few minutes before the bell. Recently she had taken to sitting on the floor by the classroom reading. She had always felt alone in registration since none of her friends shared it with her but now she felt alone.

She got to the top step of the flight and someone came from nowhere and shoved. She hadn't been paying attention, had been in the centre of the large staircase, hadn't been holding a railing. She toppled backwards, rolled over and over down the stairs, she may have screamed but by the time she smacked into the landing all the breath had been knocked from her. She was dazed, at some point, her head had hit the ground and it hurt. It hurt badly but not nearly as bad as her arm, she tried to get her breath but it hurt to breathe. She lay there in an undignified heap for what seemed like hours.

Eventually, the registration teacher arrived, it couldn't have been more than a few minutes since she fell but the panic, the pain, the inability to breathe all made it the most frightening moment of her life, tears were running down her face.

"Oh my god! What happened?" The man tried to help her up but the pain increased and she used the little breath she had to scream. She did however have the cognitive awareness to rail against the god he was calling on. "Hold on Lucia, I'm calling an ambulance."

She sobbed between shallow breaths.

ele

"I'm telling you it was Tanya!" Susan railed at the headmaster, "It has to be, she did the same stunt to me last week, I was just lucky it was on the bottom step!"

"Yeah, and she targeted our group at the ice skating on the weekend!" Jenny backed her up.

The headmaster held up his hands, "I know, I know, I'm sorry though, there were no witnesses."

"Is she going to be okay at least?" Susan asked, some of the anger leaving her.

"Well, she has a concussion, multiple fractures in her right arm and three broken ribs. Nothing too life-threatening but I doubt she will be back at school for well over a month." He admitted.

"And no one is going to be punished for this? You're going to wait until one of us is assaulted or killed? She's obviously escalating!" The anger was back, with a vengeance.

"Without proof, there isn't anything we can do, we can tell the teachers to keep an eye on her but they can't follow her around."

"Can you tell her parents what happened? Subtly suggest their daughter is a psychopath?" Susan asked, expecting him to say no.

"No, I'm sorry." Came the reply.

"Right, thanks for nothing!" She said and stormed out, her friends following her.

It was still bucketing down so they returned to their normal indoor corner in the maths department, Anne clutching her bag to her chest. "This sucks." Susan stated. "Did you ever get this Jo?"

"Nope, but I think everyone was just used to me. People don't like change." She replied sullenly.

"We should all just transfer to Mae's school." Heather suggested.

"The busses don't go that way." Abby muttered.

"We could learn to drive. Carpool." Anne suggested, quite liking the idea.

Just then Tanya approached with her full pose, "I hear your other girlfriend had an accident, how unfortunate. You lesbos need to get glasses, you all seem to be walking into things!" She said, not slowing her walk past.

"We know it was you!" Anne called after her.

Tanya replied over her shoulder, "No you don't, you just think it was me."

"She could have died!" Anne shouted.

"What a loss." Was the sarcastic reply from down the corridor.

"It fucking was her. Bitch." Susan muttered bitterly.

The girls all took the bus to the hospital after school, they had called their parents to tell them what had happened. Lucia was mainly being kept in for observation due to her concussion though the ribs were apparently a concern.

When they got to the hospital Lucia's mother met them in the foyer, she took one look at the gaggle of schoolgirls and said loudly "Out!" Pointing to the exit. "This is your fault, I don't want her near any of you!" The girls protested but a nurse gave them a glare for causing a scene so they slunk off.

Back outside they sat on covered benches near the bus stop, the rain was making a staccato drumming on the perspex overhead.

"Well, this sucks." Susan huffed. "Poor Lucia's done nothing to deserve this."

"I don't see why her mum thinks it's our fault." Heather moaned.

"Not our, my." Jo admitted quietly. Hanging her head.

"Our." Susan insisted, subtly looking at Abby and Anne. "But now she's lumping everyone in on the blame."

"I think if anyone is to blame it's her, if Lucia had been allowed to talk to us she wouldn't have been alone for this to happen." Heather said angrily.

The girls fell silent, listening to the drumming of the rain.

"When's your mum arriving?" Jo asked eventually.

"Probably another half hour. She finished work at four so it will probably take about that to get here." Susan answered.

"My dad will be here soon. He was at home today so he would have left when I sent him that text." Jenny said. "You wanting a lift?"

"I'm wanting backup." Jo admitted, "an adult to fight in Lucia's corner."

"Lucia's mum is a religious zealot. I doubt she would listen anyway." Heather spat.

"Well. Worth a try." The rain returned to centre point as the girls all got lost in their own thoughts.

Eventually, a Mercedes Pulled up, its windscreen wipers ineffectually swiping at the rain at full speed. The window rolled halfway down and Jenny's dad shouted "Who am I taking home?" Over the noise of the rain.

"We didn't get to see Lucia, her mum's being a bitch." Jenny called from the shelter of the perspex roof. "Jo was hoping you could try talking sense into her!" He nodded and the car pulled away to find a car park. They didn't see him again until Susan's mum turned up, they were just having the same conversation and asking her to intervene when he showed up, collar up and hat on against the rain.

"She is adamant that Lucia isn't allowed visitors." He shouted, the rain beating abnormally loud on the roof. "She says she's sending her to another school!"

"But... it isn't our fault some psycho bitch tried to kill her." Susan complained.

"No, it's not, it's a knee jerk reaction but she wouldn't listen to me." Jenny's dad admitted. "Now, is anyone coming home in my car?"

He took Anne, Abby and his daughter home. Susan persuaded her mum to have a try talking to the woman so she and Jo were alone for a while staring out at the rain.

"You know, I normally like the rain." Jo said, staring morosely at the sheets of water bouncing off the tarmac. "I like running in it and sitting watching it. I love thunderstorms." She twilled off, Susan didn't say anything, waiting for her to continue.

"Today it just seems depressing." She eventually finished.

Susan scooted over and gave her a hug. Cuddling up despite their wet jackets.

When eventually Susan's mum turned up they looked at her hopefully only to see her shaking her head.

"She got quite heated, the nurse suggested I leave. Sorry girls."

The drive home was morose, Susan turned the radio off after what seemed like the fifth ad break without any music in-between.

"I hope she sends her to the same school as Mae." She said to fill the silence. "They could both do with a good friend at school. It must be really hard to make friends when everyone else has been there for almost five years already."

"It took me most of those five years myself." Jo reminded her.

"Oh yeah, I'm so glad Anne made friends with you." Susan said, turning and smiling at her girlfriend in the back seat.

"Are you? If she hadn't all this wouldn't be happening." Jo reminded her.

"Hey, it would have happened eventually." She glanced at her mum and decided not to continue that tack.

"I think her mum is just looking to control her, she's probably scared she's going to lose her when she goes to university." She frowned.

"Perhaps Mae and Lucia can use that to get into the same uni as us? She could suggest that she would be close and then get a flat together in the same building as us all."

"I think perhaps you should run this grand plan past your father and I." Susan mum said ominously.

Things had been tense for weeks at school, they made sure they never went anywhere alone, Tanya always seemed to be around a corner, ready to make a snide insulting comment. There were no more physical altercations, at least no more than the odd 'accidental' collision in the corridor.

Today however there was snow on the ground. It seemed like every time they went outside a snowball hit someone in the face or the back of the head. They were convinced it was Tanya or her hangers-on but every time they looked there was no obvious culprit.

There was slush and water over every corridor, the girls were being exceptionally careful making sure they weren't pushed on steps knowing it would be easy to pass off as a slip.

Tanya was unusually snide today, comments like 'Look at the lesbians all cuddling up for warmth.' and when they were at lunch with the boys 'I thought you muffers were all man-haters, I guess some of you are just bored of bumping doughnuts.'

It was starting to get old.

It was freezing cold in the PE class, Jo wasn't sure they even had heaters in the massive gymnasium. She was doing her best to warm up by exercising but the class today was all about muscle groups and targeted exercise so there was a lot of talking and not a huge amount of doing. The teacher was using a small fibreglass dummy with no skin to point out individual muscles and then they were doing a round of whichever exercise worked that muscle, then the teacher would go around and correct people's posture and discuss why that person was not working the correct muscle. In hindsight, Jo probably would not have taken higher PE had she known it was mainly sports science and very little sport.

She did actually get a lot out of the lessons, nothing she would use in a career but it honestly helped immensely in her bodybuilding routines.

Seeing the plumes of vapour in front of people's faces the teacher felt sorry for them and sent them off around the outside of the gym with the instruction to do high steps, focusing on the stretch of the hamstrings and pointing the foot to stretch the calf.

On the third and last lap of the building, Jo was fairly far in front of the group, as she came around the last corner Tanya was standing with a number of her friends. "She even prances like a poof!" she called.

Jo had had enough, she stopped high stepping and walked right up to Tanya, through her gaggle of friends, only stopping when their noses were almost six inches apart. "What the fuck is your problem with me? Is it just homophobia or do you actually have some kind of beef that you need to get off your chest?"

By this time the rest of the class had caught up and there was quite a crowd.

"I just don't like you and your queer freak friends." Tanya spat.

"So it's just that you're a homophobic bigot? Really? Because you know that's not going to stand you well in life." Jo clenched her fist, really wanting to punch the living daylights out of her but instead turned and stalked off.

Tanya called after her, "Yeah, walk away you faggot pussy." Jo's walk slowed and she had to will herself to unclench her fists. Shaking her head she flipped her the bird and continued on to the gym where she reported the encounter to the teacher.

Support

"I'm worried, Jo hasn't come to school today." Susan fretted, "it's not like her, what if Tanya got to her somehow?" She was fidgeting as she talked to her friends, swaying from foot to foot. "I sent her a text but haven't had a reply yet."

"Do you have her home number? Perhaps she slept in?" Abby suggested, trying to placate the nervous girl.

"Yeah, hold on I'll call her, her mum doesn't go out much so she should answer." Susan got her phone out and stood off to the side to make the call. She bit her fingernails as the phone rang, on and on. Eventually, she gave up, even more concerned.

"No one answered, what does that mean? Surely it's not good?" She paced back and forth, "I spoke to her last night, she was fine, she didn't say they were going anywhere." She stopped and looked directly at Anne, "Anne, you know these things, what should I do?"

Put on the spot Anne looked at her side-eyed, "Erm, trust that she will call you when she can?" She tried.

"That's no help, perhaps I should go to their house... no, that's no use, if they didn't answer the phone there's no one home. Unless their house burnt down, would the phone still ring? What if they all died of smoke inhalation in their sleep?" Susan's pacing was getting hectic.

"Susan! Stop it!" Heather said, grabbing her shoulders and forcing her to stop pacing. "She will be fine. Honestly, there will be a perfectly sensible explanation and it won't be that they're all dead!"

Susan nodded but her eyes were still wide. "Perhaps I should find Tanya and beat it out of her, it's probably all her fault."

"Urg!" Heather threw her hands up in the air in frustration. "Jenny, your turn!"

"Nuh-uh, not unless I'm allowed to slap her." Jenny answered.

"That's it!" Susan exclaimed, grabbing her phone from her pocket, "I'll phone the hospital! If Tanya assaulted her then she will be there!"

Before any of them could persuade her not to, she had looked up the number and was on the phone, finger in her ear to block out the school noise and hunched into the wall to make herself heard.

"Thank you, yes... sorry to bother you... okay, I will, thank you so much." The girls only heard snatches of one side of the conversation. But it sounded like Susan had been transferred to another department.

"Yes, I'll hold." She gave a thumbs up to the girls, making them wonder what the hell was happening. "Jo? Oh my, I'm so glad you're there..." she walked away down the hall, the whole conversation now lost to the girls.

"What the fuck? Jo's in hospital? Shit did Tanya actually get to her?" Abby asked her friends.

"Oh man, I totally thought Susan was overreacting! I feel so stink now." Heather said, dismayed. They all fell silent, watching Susan on the phone.

— ele —

"No Susan, it's my mum, she was rushed into hospital this morning. I had to call the ambulance." Jo was leaning over the desk at the nurse's station. "Yeah, she had super bad cramps, couldn't get out of bed and she had a fever. I'm so sorry I didn't call, by the time I thought to I was in the hospital and they ask you to turn your phone off." Jo felt bad for worrying Susan so badly that she was calling the hospital. "Yeah, I came in the ambulance, dad is still at work. They're rushing her into surgery, apparently, they think it's an obstructed bowel." The nurse was looking at her with a patient stare which said 'it's not a public telephone' "Hey, Susan, can you possibly tell the office that I won't be in today? Thanks, I'd better go, I think the nurse wants to use the phone. Love you."

She hung up the phone, "Thanks, sorry for hogging it." She said to the nurse.

"It's no problem, is your dad coming in or do you need to call him?" The nurse asked, looking concerned.

"Yeah, he should be here soon. He had to go home and get clothes and stuff for mum." The nurse nodded and smiled. "He's on night shift so he probably won't stay as long as I do, he normally sleeps around this time of the day."

"That's fine, will you be okay getting home though? Your mum will probably be out of surgery in a few hours and we will know if everything went okay by then. You can wait until she wakes up but I doubt she will be compos mentis until tomorrow morning."

"Oh, I didn't think. Perhaps I should have asked my girlfriend if her dad might pick me up."

"If you want to call, just nip down to the foyer, you're allowed phones down there." The nurse suggested.

Jo wandered down the sterile corridors, she hated this place and its pale green decor but she had spent an amazing length of time here visiting her mum. She knew where to get the best awful coffee and which dishes to avoid in the cafeteria, she knew where the toilets were which had actual hand towels rather than the ineffectual hot breath hand dryers. She also knew that the most uncomfortable chairs in existence lived in the foyer. Some bright spark had apparently decided to deter people from sleeping in them by moulding them to fit absolutely nobody's arse and to be impossible to lie on without bruising your ribs and hips.

She reached the foyer and went outside rather than try the seats. She dragged her phone out of her pocket and waited impatiently for it to turn on and get a signal. The low brick wall by the door was infinitely more comfortable than the seats inside, even being just over freezing point.

Her phone eventually booted and chirped loudly about her four text messages and six missed calls, all from Susan. She smiled, it was an oddly nice feeling knowing that someone cared enough to worry. She called Susan's number from her contacts, hoping they hadn't gotten back to class yet. It answered after two rings and Susan's worried voice said "Jo, are you okay? Do you need me to come down to the hospital?"

"No, it's fine, she won't be out of the surgery until after lunch and then won't wake for a bit after that. I was just wondering if you could possibly ask one of your parents if I could get a lift? Dad's going to be sleeping by then so..."

"I'm sure they can, I will call them now and text you once I know. What ward is she in?" Susan asked. Joe gave her the information and told her she loved her again before hanging up. Suddenly she realised that today may have been the first time she said that. She considered it, sitting on the wall in the cold. She meant it, she really really meant it.

An old man sat on the wall beside her. "You okay?" He asked, Jo realised she had tears in her eyes and wiped them away.

"Yeah, happy and sad tears. It's a bit... yeah." She trailed off.

The man pulled out his cigarettes and lit one, then seeing Jo's wistful look offered her one.

"Nah, I quit a few months back, I did it for my girlfriend. She would be disappointed if I started again." It was hard, times like this she wanted to smoke so badly that her hands shook.

"Good on you, wish I had quit when I met my wife, might not have this cancer killing me!" He said cheerfully, taking another pull on the cigarette.

"Oh I'm so sorry, Are you in for treatment?" She asked.

"Nah, nothing they can do. I'm visiting my wife, she got Alzheimer's and now she has pneumonia too. The old person's friend they call it." He smiled and sighed. "At least we're pretty much going together." He looked at her and winked. "You tell that girlfriend how much you love her every chance you get. Once you get to my age those memories are the ones you hang on to." He pulled himself to his feet and stubbed out the butt against the wall, Patted Jo's shoulder and walked into the hospital.

Jo felt the tears start again, this time welling up in part for the old man.

—*ell*—

"So, how long is she likely to be in the hospital?" Susan's dad asked the nurse.

The surgery had gone well but there were likely to be follow up operations, there was talk of a colostomy bag. "You would have to speak to the surgeon but normally a full week for a bowel obstruction, if she has further surgery it could be more. She won't be on her feet for probably six weeks." The nurse explained.

Susan's dad looked at Jo, "Is your dad likely to be on shifts all that time?" Susan nodded, "well, how about you have dinner with us and then before evening visiting hours we go talk to your dad. We'll see if he would mind you staying with us for a bit."

Jo looked at the ground, willing the tears to go away. When she looked up her eyes were dry. "I think he may appreciate that."

They left the hospital and drove to their house, the conversation was sparse but Susan had sat in the back seat with her and held her hand all the way home.

"Hey honey, Jo's going to stay for dinner." Susan's dad called as he took off his jacket at the door.

"Thanks for having me Mr Niche, I really appreciate it. It was probably going to be beans on toast for tea otherwise."

"Hey, we don't know that it's not yet! Who knows what my darling Elle has cooked up for us!" He said disappearing into the kitchen.

They finished stripping off their shoes and coats and followed him. Jo was sure the dinner she smelled was not beans on toast and she was famished, not having eaten anything but a muesli bar from the vending machine.

"Dinner smells lovely Mrs N, what is it?" She asked, sincerely.

"Just spag bol Jo, nothing special. Are you girls hungry, I'm just putting the pasta on?"

Jo admitted how hungry she was and Susan's mum added some extra pasta. "By the way, just call us Rick and Elle dear, you're family now! It seems weird to be Mr and Mrs Niche."

"Okay erm, Elle, it feels a little weird though." Jo admitted.

"Well, it's Richard and Eleanor if you want a little formality but we really don't use our full names often." Elle said adding salt and oil to the pasta.

"But it is most certainly not Dick or Dicky. Got that?" Rick insisted as the girls sniggered.

The pasta, or rather the bolognese, was magnificent. Jo went back for thirds, urged on by Susan's mum, apparently she wasn't a fan of leftovers.

"So, what time will your dad be up Jo? Visiting hours are 7.30 to 9 and we want to catch him before he heads out." Rick asked, conscious that they needed to have that discussion with Jo's dad.

"He's normally up by eight, I don't know about today though. I'll send him a text and ask him to call when he wakes. Are you sure you're okay with me staying?" She asked.

"Hon, we have a spare bed, you can bus in with Susan, it makes sense." Elle insisted, "And you can visit your mum either after school or evenings, one of us can drop you and pick you up."

"Thanks, mum does like me to visit, even when I have nothing to tell her." Jo shook her head, "I guess there's no sense getting upset" she said pretty much to herself. "Susan, did you get any homework in our classes today?"

It turned out she had been given notes from a number of Jo's classes on remedial work to catch up on the day's lessons. It was mainly reading work but the girls disappeared to Susan's bedroom to study.

Jo looked around as she entered, "You know, the last time I was here was before bowling. Man, that was a good day. Felt weird wearing your clothes though."

"About that, you never gave me back the undies!" Susan teased, it obviously hit a note because Jo blushed and couldn't meet her eyes.

"Did you like them?" Susan asked with a frown, still teasing. "You know the cherries were symbolic?"

At that Jo looked up and met her eyes, "We weren't even going out!"

"Weren't we? You know bowling wasn't arranged until you showed up. Lucia made a great wingman." She couldn't keep a straight face any longer and burst out laughing. "Oh man, the look on your face!"

They knuckled down after that, Susan only helping Jo a few times, there obviously hadn't been any earth-shattering topics covered and they had pretty much finished by the time Jo's dad called.

"Rick, damn that still feels weird to call you that, erm, my dad says he plans to leave at 7.45 so if you want to talk to him we should leave." So announced. "We've done our homework so we are ready when you are."

"No time like the present." he said and hopped up from the couch. "You got everything in case your dad says no?"

They got round to Jo's with loads of time spare, Susan felt bad about the fact she was nervous about leaving the car outside. It wasn't that bad a neighbourhood and her dad didn't seem to care. She felt like she was insulting her girlfriend by distrusting the neighbours.

Jo opened the door and called, "Dad, Susan and her dad are here." They walked down the hall and found him finishing his breakfast, hurriedly he swallowed his mouthful and wiped his hands, getting up to shake Rick's hand.

Rick introduced himself, "I'm sorry to hear about your wife, Jo tells me the surgery went well though?" Jo's dad had been on the phone with the surgeon in the afternoon so he was well informed. "We were just wondering if you wanted us to look after Jo for the week? I thought it might give you one less thing to worry about." Rick asked.

Jo's dad looked at her, noting the hopeful look on her face. "Hmmm, this isn't an excuse to get close with your girlfriend is it?" He asked her jokingly.

"She would be in the spare bedroom." Rick explained, "and we would drop and pick her up from the hospital for visiting hours. It just means you don't need to cook for her or worry about her alone in the house."

"Yeah, it's actually a really nice thing for you to do, I'm sure Jo will appreciate it as much as I do." He waved a hand to the kitchen seats, "Have a seat, I hope you don't mind me finishing my breakfast in front of you?" He sat and picked up his fork. "Chop chop Jo, go pack, don't keep them waiting. And remember your guitar."

Susan and Jo rushed off to her room, leaving the men to talk.

"Now that we're alone, is everything okay? Is your wife alright?" Rick asked.

"Yeah, it sounds a bit more serious than the other times she's been in hospital but she'll pull through, she's tough." He finished his breakfast and got up to wash his plate.

"Is there anything else at all I can do to help?" Rick asked, feeling a little helpless.

"Just look after Jo, that's actually a big help. She looks and acts tough, and I wouldn't say she's fragile by any means, but she is still a teenager. She needs support, more than I can give her at the moment."

He had just finished washing up as the girls reappeared heavily laden with bags. "Got everything, toothbrush? Good, well better head out then."

They walked down the hall, Jo's dad turning lights off behind them. Somehow it felt foreboding, like they were leaving for a lot longer than the week.

Jo ended up staying three weeks, she had quickly fallen into a routine. She ran from school to the hospital and stayed for afternoon visiting hours, Rick then picked her up and they had dinner before either Elle took her to the gym or she headed out for a long run. And then she spent some time with her dad on the weekend.

Elle's gym buddies were all amazed at the weight she lifted, unlike at school the gym Susan's mum went to had weight machines rather than free weights. This was both good and bad, it meant that she didn't need a spotter but she had to change her routine entirely. Susan had come with them a few times but had found she didn't enjoy weight lifting, and she certainly didn't enjoy her mum's centergy or body balance classes.

She had been a little annoyed at herself, having really wanted to join in this aspect of Jo's life.

"It doesn't matter." Jo had said, "it's probably healthier not to be in each other's pockets 24/7 anyway!"

She was probably right but at the moment, even though they were living together it seemed she hardly saw Jo! She did enjoy getting serenaded every evening though, as did her parents and the bedtime kisses were nice. Somehow they were never alone. All she wanted to do was have a nice long snogging session, perhaps a little more, but her parents were always there, always watching, it was so unfair.

"So swimming tomorrow." Susan commented, knowing Jo had been nervous about it. "Did you get the swim shirt from Kelly?"

Jo stopped plucking the guitar strings, "Yeah, it's a little tight around the shoulders though."

"But you're comfortable in it?" Jo asked gently.

"Yeah, it looks pretty cool with my board shorts. I'm looking forward to this, I haven't been swimming in years." She assured her girlfriend.

"Cool, we're going to the big pool with the water slides too. I love that place." She smiled, "perhaps we can go down one of the slides together?"

Jo smiled back, "I would love that, I've actually never been to that pool. We always went to the local one for swimming lessons."

"So, you haven't been on the slides?" Jo shook her head, "What never? Any slides?"

"Just that open-topped yellow one they used to have at the side of the little pool. The one they took down after a couple of kids fell off it." Jo admitted.

"Oh, this is going to be so great! You're going to love it!" Susan said, almost vibrating in her seat.

The next day they all met at the pool in the morning, they had timed it for the slides opening at ten. Mae was last to arrive and when she finally showed up they went inside the huge complex, it seemed about ten times larger than the local pool and had three interconnected pools, one of which had a wave machine, and a gym, a sauna and steam room, hot pools and of course the slides which you could see weaving in and out of the building from the outside. There was even a set of indoor courts for netball and badminton and a couple of squash courts.

"We should totally play squash some time! That is so much fun!" Heather squealed.

They made their way through to the changing rooms, to a number of the girls' relief there was actually a small line of changing cubicles, not that they needed them on the way in, everyone had their swimsuits on under their clothes.

They hurriedly threw their belongings into lockers, everyone in a rush to get to the pool.

There was a short blast from a high pitched klaxon, "Come on, that noise means the wave pool's about to start!" Kelly said, dragging her sister's arm.

They all followed along and jumped into the lovely warm water. Right enough, just as they got in the water it seemed to retract, everyone falling by about a meter then with a brief delay there was a surge. They all screamed as the water lifted them high in the air. Jo grabbed at her girlfriend in panic, feeling instantly out of her depth.

"It's okay, I've got you, just tread water." Once she got over the panic, Jo realized it wasn't that hard. "Okay, let's go to the wall over there, we can hang onto the rope."

Holding the rope felt safer but it highlighted the difference in depth when the waves peaked and troughed. Both Jo and Susan squealed riding the waves then Susan screamed for real as Kelly surfaced unexpectedly from under the water right in front of them..

"Holy crap Kelly, you scared the shit out of me!" She complained. "I can't believe you swim underwater in the waves." Kelly laughed and used the rope to jump backwards high out of the water as the wave receded.

Abby and Anne were holding hands out in the shallow end, enjoying being able to put their feet down when the waves receded.

"Your sister certainly loves the water." Abby said, seeing her jump into the air.

"My sister just loves to be the centre of attention." They weathered the next wave, "where did Heather and Mae go?"

They looked around but didn't see the pair anywhere. "Perhaps they don't like the waves?"

They looked around and saw the reason their friends had disappeared, boys. They were floating around the river ride with Brian and one of his friends, "I suspect it wasn't a coincidence those two being here!" Anne said to her girlfriend, whooping as the next wave unexpectedly lifted them both off their feet, an undertow current pulling them into deeper water.

They played in the waves until the machine shut off, all of them gaining confidence as they got used to the waves but still using it as an excuse to hold hands.

"This is so cool, come on Anne, let's go down the slide together!" Kelly insisted, once again hauling on her sister's arm.

"Okay, okay, I think everyone wants to go on the slides, there's no rush!" Anne said, giving Abby an apologetic glance.

"Yes, there is, we can get there before the queue!" Kelly said, still hauling her arm.

Anne allowed herself to be led to the steel steps up to the slides, there were already people in front of them but Kelly had been right, the queue at the top was minimal but looking back there was a line of people climbing the steps behind them.

"Let's go on the dark one, and let's turn so we're going backwards on our backs! It's super scary that way!" Anne laughed at the exuberance but conceded to Kelly's wishes.

As they entered Kelly whispered, "Wait till the first bend, if they can't see they won't tell us off!"

They started out sitting with Kelly sitting in front of Anne, sitting bolt upright. As they gathered speed and passed the first bend Kelly demonstrated the turn only just visible in the gloom, ending up heading downward stretched out head first. Anne did her best to emulate her but managed to get a foot in the face, she did get the right orientation though and Kelly clamped her legs around her, whooping in the dark tube. She had been right, it was the scariest slide she had ever been on.

They hit the water at the end full tilt, their heads ploughing under the foot deep water. Anne got up coughing and spluttering. "Wow, that was so cool!"

"I know right? Don't let them catch you doing it though. My friend got kicked off the slide when they caught her."

"I'm totally taking Abby on that slide, she would love it." Anne said, just as Jo and Susan came shooting out the other tube beside them.

"That was awesome!" Jo exclaimed, "Man, I didn't know what I was missing out on! Let's go again!" She pulled her girlfriend up the stairs in front of Kelly, to her annoyance.

"Races!" Kelly called, "There are four slides, we each take one and the first out wins!" She called.

"You're on!" Jo said as the girls ran up the stairs.

By the time they tired of the sides, Jo was the only one not complaining of aching legs from climbing the steps. "You guys need to do more trail running!" She boasted.

The girls had planned on all sitting in the hot tub but the sign declared '16 and over', they tried to smuggle Kelly in but a nosy obese man complained. In the end, they took turns to soak in the jacuzzi, whilst some of them played on the inflatables in the big pool with Kelly.

"We should sit in the steam room." Susan suggested, "I would quite like to see Jo all sweaty." She teased,

"We'll make her glisten,

And gleam,

And with massage,

And just a little bit of ste-e-am, haha,

She'll be pink and quite clean,

She'll be a strong woman" she paraphrased from rocky horror. "Seriously though, I would love to see those abs all glistening."

"Get a room!" Heather said, not that she was one to talk, all cuddled up to Brian in the hot pool. Mae seemed to be getting along well with his friend too.

Jo gave a shifty little look around and smiled before leading her girlfriend to the steam room. It wasn't as fun as Susan had expected though, it was exceptionally hot and fairly crowded. After about five minutes of sitting side by side in silence, they gave up and tried the sauna. They failed completely at the sauna, neither of them had brought a towel and they quickly realised that the wood was so hot you couldn't sit on it.

"Well, that sucked." Susan admitted, "I had a completely different idea of how that was going to go!"

Jo grabbed her hand before she could walk off and pulled her into a loose hug. "I think someone needs a cold shower!" She said cheekily before surreptitiously pressing the button on the cold shower they were standing under. Susan screamed and tried in vain to escape, squirming in Jo's laughing embrace for a few seconds before the shower shut off.

Fortunately, she saw the funny side and she enjoyed jumping back into the pool which seemed so much hotter after the cold shower.

Eventually, they had to leave, everyone's fingers and toes were wrinkled like prunes and they were all hungry and thirsty. Agreeing to meet the boys outside they traipsed into the showers, Abby however held back Anne and Kelly.

"Now, I said there would be a test, this is it. I want you both to shower and change in the communal area, I'm going to be watching you, no staring and no obviously averting your gaze. Remember, eye contact, act natural." She whispered to them before letting them go.

The girls all showered together, Abby kept an eye on her students and was very pleased with their progress right up until Jo took off her shirt. "Kelly! Stop drooling, shut your mouth." She hissed.

Kelly quickly averted her eyes and apologized, "But you're like a bodybuilder, you can see every muscle." She said shyly.

"Well, that's because I am a bodybuilder, I just don't go to shows and paint myself bronze!" Jo explained, surprisingly not seeming too self-conscious.

"Strike a pose!" Kelly asked excitedly.

"No!" Jo said but she turned around and flexed her broad shoulders anyway, her muscles standing out under her skin.

"Wow! That is so hot!" Kelly exclaimed before flaming her hand over her own mouth. "Sorry." She squeaked.

"Hey, that's my girlfriend your ogling, I'm the only one allowed to lust after her!" Susan laughed.

"Seriously though Jo, would you consider modelling for me?" Abby asked, "You can have your clothes on, or at least underwear on. You just don't get to draw muscles like that in real life."

Jo was quite obviously blushing now and rather than answer threw her scrunchy at Abby before rinsing off and heading into the changing rooms with her towel.

"Wow, I wish I had her body." Abby said wistfully.

"I've seen what she does to get those muscles. There's no way you could have the willpower to keep that up." Susan said, "But god yes, I do love her body!" She said in a low voice before chasing off after Jo.

The rest of the time in the changing room went well, Anne and Kelly managing to maintain a normal level of decorum.

◦◦◦

After meeting up with the boys they took the bus to their normal cafe.

They came through the door laughing and having fun only to fall silent when they caught sight of their friend sitting alone at a small corner table. Lucia looked small with the large cast still on her arm. Looking around to make sure Lucia's parents weren't around Susan ran over to the table and gave her friend a big hug, tears leaking from her eyes. Lucia winced at the hug, the watchers couldn't be sure if it was pain from the broken ribs or the fear of being spotted with her friend.

"Oh my god, I've missed you so much." Susan sobbed, not letting go of the hug. "I'm so sorry. My timing was awful and I should have told you first. You're my best friend and you deserved to be the first one I told. This is all my fault." Susan's words devolved into unintelligible sobs. As Lucia just rubbed her back, unshed tears glistening in her eyes.

"Come on guys, let's give them some space." Abby said, leading them through the shop to a large table at the other side of the room.

As she passed Jo squeezed Susan's shoulder and said, "Both of you come to join us once you're ready. If you want."

It was about ten minutes before Susan returned to the group alone, tears still in her eyes. "Her parents are coming to collect her soon so she can't come over." She sniffed and accepted a tissue from Mae. "She starts school with you on Monday Mae. Can you look after her? Please?"

"Of course." Mae said, gripping Susan's hand on the table. "We're already good friends, perhaps she can come and hang out with me and Heather after school too."

Susan nodded. "We talked about university. Her mum wants her close! What irony! Perhaps you two could share a flat?"

"I would like that." Mae assured her. "Have you all got your applications in?"

They spent the next half hour chatting, briefly hiding Susan when Lucia's parents came in but essentially just reiterating their dreams for next year.

ELATION

Before any of the girls were ready the mid-year practice exams came round. It was the week before the Christmas holidays and there was snow on the ground. The halls of the school were crowded with children staying indoors, icy blasts of wind came every time someone opened an exterior door and they were all bundled up with jackets, scarves and gloves.

"I think they're getting the hardest exams out of the way first, that English exam was brutal." Jo complained. "I'm really not looking forward to the maths one tomorrow."

"Well, I have chemistry this afternoon, it should be fun." Anne said, enthusiastically.

"Only you could say a science exam would be fun. You are such a geek!" Heather teased.

"Well, I have the afternoon off so I'm going to go home and study. I really need to ace these exams." Jo said dejectedly.

"Want a study partner? I have the afternoon free too and I'm pretty good at maths." Susan asked.

They headed off together to the bus stop.

"So, she's back living at home? Any idea how her mum is?" Heather asked.

"Not great." Anne said sadly, "she's still recovering from the last operation and they are talking about bringing her in for another one. Susan said they are having them around to their house for Christmas dinner because Jo's mum isn't up for cooking. Or shopping, or wrapping. Apparently getting out of bed to the toilet is hard enough. Jo is helping out around the house and her dad is doing most of the cooking."

"Oh man, that must be hard on her. Hopefully, it won't affect her grades, she's really pinning her hopes on this scholarship." Heather sympathised.

"Yeah, these mid-year exams are important for all of us, apparently the conditional offers are mainly done on the mid-year results." Anne reminded them, resulting in groans from Heather and Abby.

Over the week the girls got more and more flustered, the exams making them realise how much they hadn't recalled from class and causing panicked late-night study sessions. They were fairly burnt out by Thursday.

"So, last exams tomorrow. I've got computing and statistics, what do you guys have?" Anne asked.

They went around the group and almost nobody had the same exams, the last day had obviously been reserved for the optional classes and they had all taken slightly different options.

"I am so glad this week is almost over. I feel like I haven't slept all week." Indeed, all the girls looked like they had bags under their eyes. The boys they were having lunch with however, all seemed to be loving the relaxed schedule. It seemed like they weren't taking the exams seriously at all.

"Let's do something this weekend. Let off steam. We could bring movie night forward? Or squash? You said that was fun." Anne suggested.

"That's a good idea. We could do both. Does everyone have non-marking trainers?" Heather asked, the school required indoor gym shoes to be non-marking so in essence she was basically just reminding them to take them home. "We have at least four racquets at home so we just need to book the courts."

There was a feeling of celebration on Saturday, all the exams were over and school was out for the holidays. In the morning there had been a thick shimmering sheet of frost over everything with a clear sky and not a breath of wind, it had truly felt Christmassy.

By the time it came close to their court booking in the afternoon the frost had melted and the day felt only mildly nippy. The girls met again outside the pool building, smiling and happy. Susan and Heather were both wearing cute little tennis dresses while everyone else had opted for shorts and t-shirts.

"So, I take it the dresses mean you two play a few racquet sports?" Jo asked.

"Well, Heather plays squash a bit but I only play tennis sometimes in the summer. My mum just liked the dress." Susan explained.

"Okay girls, we're going to play on two courts, left court winner stays on, right court loser stays on. That is, until you're too tired." Heather said, taking charge. She explained the rules and showed them the serve before retreating upstairs to watch with Jo and Mae who had opted to watch for a match or two.

They started warming up, and warming the ball up, "Come on, hit it hard, flick the wrist, get the ball moving, if you don't hit it hard it won't warm up!" Heather called from the balcony. The girls below were struggling to get the ball to come back past the line. "Come on, smash it!"

Eventually, the balls warmed up and started bouncing further, the girls were probably also getting the hang of having to hit it hard, unlike tennis. "Okay, we're going to start. It's new rules so you don't have to be on your serve to win a point okay? Geeze why am I asking, you guys never watched squash in your lives." Heather was getting quite animated.

They played the first games to eleven, ignoring the two clear points rule. The girls then swapped out and Jo and Mae went in. Once people got the hang of the game it was hectic, sprinting front to back and side to side. The second games lasted longer and the two girls who had played both games decided they were not staying on, both of them were breathing heavily. Heather had been coaching, scoring and refereeing both matches and handed the task off to Kelly who thought she had at least the coaching part down. Shouting 'Return to the T' constantly seemed to be all that part consisted of.

Heather had decided to play Jo, she had been watching all the girls and whilst Jo didn't have the hand-eye coordination to put the ball in the desired location each shot, she was reaching the ball and making a return consistently.

She started off with a serve straight to where Jo was standing, Jo returned the shot and Heather effortlessly reached and returned it, straight to the furthest point on the court. Jo managed to get to that ball too, with a heroic effort which ended in her smashing into the wall. Heather stepped to the shot and casually returned it to the back corner, furthest away from Jo who didn't even try to get to the ball.

The girls who were watching all cheered, amazed at how easy Heather was making the game look. She continued to trounce Jo thoroughly, ending the game eleven nil and by the end of the game, the other girls had stopped their game and were watching rapt from the balcony.

"Now, do you see what I did?" Heather asked, "I returned to the T, every single shot. Watch, see, two steps from here to the corner, two back. Even if Jo returns the ball to the same place, I can still get there and return it." The girls were all nodding. "Good, now go try it. I'm going to play Jo a couple more times, she isn't winded yet."

She proceeded to play another three games with Jo, each one Jo managed a little better, there were more volleys at least but the games still ended eleven nil.

"Good game." Heather said, patting Jo on the shoulder. Jo was breathing harder than she did during speed training, harder than she ever breathed doing uphills on the trails.

She looked at Heather in amazement. "How are you not wrecked?"

"Well, you still aren't getting back to the T consistently and your shots are not targeted to make me move. You're getting there though, perhaps you should come to a practice night sometime?" She said as they vacated the room for the other girls.

By the end of their hour booking, most of the girls were sweaty and tired. They showered and changed before taking the bus to Anne's house.

"Sorry girls, no pizza tonight. It's going to be too damned cold out." Pete apologised. "It's pasta night instead, I've done a cheesy macaroni and pesto shells."

The girls tucked in with gusto, the squash had built up a hunger. They all talked animatedly about their games, Pete and Jane listening intently.

As they all filtered upstairs for the movie Pete stopped Anne, "Hey, I just wanted to say thank you. It's really good of you to include your sister like you have this year. She really loves spending time with you and your friends." He ruffled her hair and sent her off to watch sixth sense, wondering at the twist of fate that had made her include Kelly more in her life.

On Christmas eve Jo and her parents stayed the night at the Niche's house. For the first time ever Jo and Susan had been allowed to share a bed, under the strict provisor that there be no nookie happening. Elle had even insisted that the door be left open and had threatened that Santa wouldn't come if they were bad!

Christmas eve had been special, the two families had sung Christmas carols, Jo playing along on the guitar, and they had played silly party games, charades and Pictionary. There had been mulled wine and

Christmas cake and an assortment of things they only got to eat at Christmas. It had absolutely felt like the best Christmas ever and it wasn't even Christmas day.

And now Jo was playing big spoon in her girlfriend's bed. She was in heaven, if heaven was a place you loved to be but absolutely couldn't sleep.

She was warm and comfortable, enjoying listening to the soft breathing of her girlfriend in her arms and the smell of her shampoo. She was feeling content and mellow. She just had no idea why sleep just wouldn't come. She had tried counting Susan's breaths, of thinking of a candle flame and feeding each errant thought into the flame, she had even tried consciously relaxing each muscle of her body from the toes up. Nothing had worked. That said, perhaps it was just because she was enjoying the moment so much she subconsciously wanted to make it last.

She smiled when she heard Mrs Niche being Santa Claus, she had slipped in through the open door and gently set two pillowcases at the foot of the bed, obviously not realising Jo was awake as she stood at the door and smiled at them cuddling in the bed.

Shortly after that, she must have finally fallen asleep as the next thing she knew Susan was stroking her thigh to wake her up gently. "Hey, gorgeous. It's breakfast time."

Jo blinked her eyes open groggily. "Mmm, kiss?" She asked, seeing Susan inches away. She drew her in for a long steamy kiss.

"Merry Christmas." She said with a smile.

There was a cough from the door. "You two getting up? Perhaps you should!" Jo's mum said, leaning heavily on her walking sticks. "Before you get carried away." There was humour in her voice.

The girls laughed and sat up in bed. "Merry Christmas mum." Jo said.

"Merry Christmas, now, how about you help your old mum down the stairs?" Jo climbed out of bed and gave her mum a hug before lifting

her bodily and walking carefully down the stairs, her mum laughing all the way.

As they got to the kitchen Susan's mum asked cheekily, "So, did Santa leave you anything last night or were you two bad girls?"

"Presents!" Jo exclaimed, having completely forgotten. She ran back up the stairs and hugged Susan again! "Presents!" She said, squeezing her tight.

"Argh! Too... tight!" Susan squealed. Jo released her and pecked her on the lips. "Love you. Want to take these presents downstairs and see what 'Santa' got us?"

They dragged the sacks downstairs with them, still in their pyjamas, to sit on the floor in the living room in front of the tree.

Their parents sat on the couches with coffees and bucks fizz, happily watching them tear into their presents.

They had loads of tiny wrapped gifts, chocolates and sweets which they opened and shared around, small games and socks, each gift opened and cooed over every single one, each item appreciated. Jo paused watching Susan open her gifts whilst she ate an entire individually wrapped satsuma.

"Ooh! A book, on dead tree! 'A time travelling tank?' I've never heard of that one." Susan said, pausing to read the first few pages.

"It might be a bit young for you but someone at the gym wrote it." Susan's mum said, worriedly breaking the 'Santa' charade.

"Cool, got to support the indie writers!" Susan said, putting the book aside for later.

"Awesome, a new compass!" Jo said, testing magnetic north.

"I saw your one had all the directions worn off." Her mum admitted.

Their haul of little gifts grew and the pile of wrapping paper grew faster. When they had finished they both hugged all the adults, thanking them for the presents.

"My turn for gifts?" Jo asked, not waiting for an answer. She pulled out a stack of identical-looking presents and carefully handed them to the correct people. They tore into them to reveal identical CDs.

"Now, I have to admit, the covers are all the same because I didn't want Abby to do too much work on my gifts." The cover was a sketch of Jo, done in broad dark strokes in ink, she was holding a guitar, the minimal strokes giving it a ghostlike impression.

"It's beautiful, she's very talented." Jo's dad complimented.

"The tracklist is different on each of them, a few songs are repeated because a lot of you like the same music and it saved me a lot of time." They each turned the case over and were surprised at her knowledge of their music taste.

"That's very thoughtful of you Jo, here let's put mine on." Rick said, putting the CD in the machine. He was surprised to hear Jo's voice, accompanied only by guitar, playing his favourite Joe Cocker song.

"Oh wow, I was just expecting a mixtape. This is amazing, you recorded all these songs? When?" He asked.

"It was my music project this term, I recorded a few songs each class. You've likely heard them all since I practised them all here."

Rick gave her a big hug. "This is such an amazing gift. We will be listening to nothing but Jo all day today, I want to hear all these albums!" He declared. The rest of the adults all hugged and thanked her for the amazing gifts before Susan got out a box filled with her gifts for people.

"Okay, these are nothing compared to Jo's presents but I had a lot of pocket money saved up." She handed the first one to Jo's mum.

She unwrapped it and found a kindle. "Now, it's second hand but it's pristine. I've loaded it with crime mystery novels for you too."

"Oh darling, it's perfect! Come give me a hug." She said, her eyes glistening. "You girls are so wonderful."

"Okay this one is heavy, again it isn't brand new but Jo assures me it's good." She hefted a weighty box and handed it to Jo's dad. "We may have... borrowed your one to check the holes were right." He pulled out a bowling ball from the box. "They filled and redrilled the thumb hole."

He stood up and hefted the ball for weight, putting his fingers in the holes and swinging the ball back one forth. "It's great, and my old one is awful. I feel bad you spending all your money on me though."

"Hey, since meeting your daughter I've spent almost none of my pocket money. It was burning a hole in my pocket. Anyway, everything I bought was second hand and at a good price." She assured him.

Next, she handed her mom a gift, the wrapping was off almost before Susan had let go. It was a Delia Smith cookbook. "Oh wow, this is your gran's cookbook, the one I love."

"No, it's a copy. I didn't just go steal grans cookbook! Oh shit, we haven't told gran." Susan realised. "She's going to call tonight. So you think she's going to be okay when I introduce Jo?"

"She'll be fine. I may have... primed her a little already." The look of relief on Susan's face was priceless.

Her dad was given a boring old computer game, wings 64 for his retro games console. Susan had no doubt they would be playing the blocky old thing before lunch.

"And Jo." She said, handing her a small box.

Jo unwrapped it carefully. "What is it?" She asked looking at the clear case in puzzlement.

"Oh, oops, that was meant to be the second one." Susan apologized, handing Jo an identical-looking parcel.

This time she recognised the contents, "A GoPro? Wow, these are cool."

"The other bit is a waterproof case with a thing to attach it to your bag. I thought it would be cool if you could record some of your runs and bike rides." Susan explained, nervous that her girlfriend didn't like it.

"It's wonderful." Jo said, hugging her tightly. "This is the best Christmas ever."

"But wait, there's more! As the advert says." Rick said, reaching down to get a little box from beside the sofa. "Now, this is a very big present from all of us to both of you. Before I give you this I have to say, it is a very big investment and we are putting a lot of trust in you giving you this."

He handed the box to Jo.

The girls looked at them in confusion, then looked at the plain cardboard box, frowning. "What is it?" Susan asked.

"Well, open it and find out." Elle said, excitedly.

Jo tore the tape off the top and reached in, she pulled out a brightly coloured ring of keys for baby's teething and looked at Susan confused.

"Oh no, you're having another baby?" Susan asked wide-eyed.

"No! Look further!" Her dad said.

Jo fished about in the box and pulled out a photograph. It was a picture of a high rise building with a single flat highlighted in permanent marker.

"You can't see inside yet, and you can't get the real keys because someone is already renting it but we've bought you a flat to use during university. The plastic keys were your dad's idea." Elle explained.

The girls' screams were ear piercing, they hugged each other and jumped up and down.

"Susan's mum and dad put in most of the money, we just chipped in for the down payment." Jo's dad said, wanting to make that clear.

Jo pulled her mum to her feet and hugged her, pulling her dad up too for a group hug, before long everyone was included.

It had been a long day, Anne's feet and hands were icy and her gloves were soaked through. The girls had all met up in town for coffee again, all excitedly talking about Christmas this time Kelly hadn't come, she was actually hanging out with her own friends. They had done a secret Santa as they had for many years and exchanged small gifts, many of them hand made.

After the coffee shop, they had visited an art gallery, something Abby had virtually had to blackmail them into. It had been surprisingly fun, in Anne's opinion none of the art had been as good as Abby's work. Especially the ongoing piece she was doing. It had taken a lot of courage to pose naked but the picture of her back silhouetted at the window was turning out beautifully. She still wasn't sure if she wanted anyone else to see it through.

It had taken a surprisingly long time to walk around the gallery, the place was a maze filled with paintings, textiles and sculpture and they had paused numerous times to discuss, and sometimes laugh at, the art exhibits. There were a number which Anne swore must have been done by five-year-olds, the price tags underneath however said otherwise!

"You should get your paintings in here." Anne had suggested, "Look at this, two thousand! And it's awful!"

Abby had just laughed, "They don't exhibit teenagers' work here. You have to be an actual artist." she had said, not relenting when Anne insisted she was better than most of these 'artists'.

"Nah, the best I could do is a coffee shop wall. Perhaps I could talk to Lucia's friend." she paused, obviously considering the idea. "I would need to do some generic stuff, most of my recent work has been pictures of you."

This caused Anne to blush.

On the way out Abby had stopped to buy a book, "Photography?" Anne asked her, "Are you wanting to get into that?" The book was titled, 'Photography, beyond auto'.

"Well, dad has an old SLR camera that he says I can use and there's a whole term on photography and developing film this year in art, I want to get ahead." she explained.

"Dad's got an old Fuji digital SLR that he hardly uses. I'm sure he wouldn't mind me borrowing it, I think it would be cool to take some arty shots. Perhaps we could have a photography date?" Anne suggested.

"You might have to read my new book!" Abby teased.

"We could read it together, like we did with the homework. I liked that." Anne suggested, biting her lip. Abby just smiled and led her outside.

The other girls were waiting impatiently for them outside in the thick snow, "How about we go to the park and build a snowman?" Heather had suggested. This was why Anne's fingers now felt like they would fall off.

The snowman had grown to be about seven feet tall with four balls of decreasing size. Heather and Mae had insisted on singing 'Do you want to build a snowman?' constantly, even with the other girls trying to persuade them to try other songs. Jo in particular did a hauntingly beautiful verse from 'Walking in the air' which echoed off the surrounding hills.

"Abby, can we go home? I'm freezing." Anne eventually asked her girlfriend, shivering and stomping her feet.

"Yeah, sure. We'll just say goodbye." She said, wandering over to the other girls who were carving details into the huge snowman.

The girls all tried to get them to stay, insisting they could go back to the coffee shop or somewhere else to get warm but Abby was thinking about snuggling into bed with a hot water bottle and a book so she declined.

On the bus ride home, they cuddled in for warmth, eliciting smiles from a couple of old women riding the bus. Anne briefly wondered how some old people could be so accepting of gay relationships before realising they probably just didn't associate girls hugging with lesbian relationships.

They were warming up a little by the time the bus pulled into their stop. The heaters had been on full blast at their feet and Anne was getting pins and needles as the blood flow returned.

"Come on, let's run." Abby said, dragging Anne's hand. "It will warm you up."

Anne reluctantly broke into a run, covering the short distance to Abby's house quickly. "I really hope your dad has the fire going." she said, blowing on her fingers as Abby fumbled the keys with gloved hands.

"Nope, they're both out." She got the door unlocked and stomped the snow off her boots before stepping into the dark house.

"We do have loads of hot water bottles and wheat bags though." she said, pulling off her gloves and then removing her jacket and boots. "Man, my trousers are soaked too."

Anne shuffled in and closed the door, having kicked the snow off her own shoes. She paused in taking her jacket off as Abby started

stripping her trousers off. She was captivated by how cute her girlfriend looked in just her jumper and undies.

"Come on, stop perving and get out of those wet things!" Abby said, kicking her back into gear.

She took off her outdoor clothes and paused before deciding to also remove her socks and trousers.

Abby smiled, it looked a little predatory to Anne but she just took her wet things and carried them through the kitchen to the drier.

"Come on, there's a heated floor in the kitchen, it's lovely on your feet." Abby beckoned.

She stood uncomfortably, hands in front of her undies as Abby busied herself boiling the kettle and microwaving the wheat packs.

"What's got you all shy?" Abby asked, noticing how she was standing. "It's not like I haven't seen you in your underwear before."

"I don't know. It just seems... different." Anne said, unsure herself why she felt so awkward.

Abby shrugged and turned back to the microwave, pulling out and tossing a wheat bag to Anne. She caught it and juggled it hand to hand, waiting for it to cool down enough to hold.

"You can go snuggle up in my bed if you like, I'll be up as soon as the kettle boils." Abby suggested, wrapping her own wheat bag in a tea towel. "Want tea? There should be enough water."

Anne said yes to the tea and then wandered up to Abby's room. She paused before she got under the covers, worrying her lower lip, then decided to be brave and took off her jumper. Hopping into bed in just her underwear she pushed the wheat bag down to her feet and lay there in a fetal position shivering.

It seemed like forever before Abby came up carrying a tray. She set it down on her chest of drawers and handed Anne two hot water bottles

before taking the book and mugs and setting them on her bedside table.

Before she got into the bed she noticed Anne's jumper on the floor, "Ooh, we're doing that are we?" she said cheekily and stripped her top and bra off.

Anne's breath stuck in her throat and her eyes widened.

"Right enough they are a bit cold!" Abby said, rubbing her breasts and then hugging the wheat pack to her chest and shivering. "Budge up."

Anne realised she was holding her breath and forced herself to breathe whilst scooting back in the bed. She reached behind herself and unhooked her bra, pulling it out from the covers and discretely dropping it at the other side of the bed. She then hugged a hot water bottle to her chest, its furry cover tickling her bare skin.

Abby got in the bed, sitting upright and kicking the bottle down to her feet. "Well, sit up, you can't drink tea lying down."

Anne scooted upwards, clutching the duvet to her chest. "Here you go, I added lemon and honey. I hope that's okay?"

Anne nodded, not trusting herself to speak, she was exceedingly nervous, in bed with her girlfriend in a house with no adults she felt something had to happen.

They sipped the tea, not saying much, it was delicious and the mug warmed their hands nicely. Once they finished Abby took the mugs and set them on the bedside table.

"How do you want to do this? The way we did it last time would leave me out of the covers and all cold!" Abby asked.

Anne didn't answer, just scooted over and put her head in the crook of Abby's arm, resting on her shoulder. "Right, that should work." Abby agreed, opening the book.

Anne was glad, so far she had avoided baring herself to Abby today, for some reason she just felt extremely shy.

As they read Abby hand came to rest on top of Anne's breast, the covers the only thing separating them.

The book was short with many pictures illustrating the effects of focus and aperture and various other settings. When they were almost finished reading the book Anne noticed the page droop towards the bed. She glanced at Abby and realised her friend had fallen asleep reading. Not wanting to disturb her she nestled her head down into her girlfriend's shoulder and draped her arm softly across her stomach, enjoying the unobstructed feel of her girlfriend's skin. Within seconds she too fell asleep.

Anne woke to find her hand had moved in her sleep and now she had a hard nipple poking between her fingers. She lay, listening, trying to decide whether Abby's parents had gotten home yet. As she did Abby smiled, "Mind if I move my hand to a similar place?" she asked without opening her eyes. When Anne made a little noise of acceptance she moved her hand from outside the cover to underneath, the cold skin of her arm from being outside the covers was a slight shock and Anne tensed up. Abby didn't move a muscle until she felt Anne relax.

"You okay?" she asked, nervously.

"Mmm-hmm." Anne replied meekly.

"We don't have to do anything if you don't want to." she assured her.

"No, I...I do, just...perhaps what you said that night. You know, when I told you about Jo's suggestion?" Anne trailed off into a whisper.

"Hmm, really? That would be pretty hot." Abby agreed, rolling over to give her girlfriend a kiss. "You sure?"

Anne nodded and came in for a deeper kiss, her hands roaming more freely on her girlfriend's body.

They kissed and fumbled for a while, enjoying the new level of intimacy before Anne broke off. She looked at Abby and nodded, Abby returned the nod, fingers disappearing into her own underwear.

Abby was getting fairly into it when she noticed Anne was frowning, "Are you okay?" she asked.

"You look like you're enjoying it, keep going." Anne insisted but the moment was lost.

"No, what's wrong?" Abby asked again, concerned for her friend.

"I just... it's meant to... I don't know, it just isn't doing anything." Anne admitted, tears forming in her eyes.

"Oh Anne, come here!" Abby said, pulling her into a hug.

"There's something wrong with me!" Anne sobbed into her girlfriend's bare shoulder.

"No! There's nothing wrong, Anne, there's nothing wrong, hear me?" Abby was rubbing circles on her back. "You like kissing right? And the touching? You like touching don't you?" Anne nodded into her shoulder, tears running freely down her face. "Well, perhaps you just don't like doing it yourself?" Anne sniffed and shrugged. "Perhaps next time we just... keep going? See what happens?" Anne sniffed again and nodded.

Abby held her until the tears stopped. "Shall we get cleaned up and go downstairs? Perhaps some chocolate will make things seem better? I've got that Terry's Chocolate Orange that mum bought me for Christmas."

Anne nodded and hugged her tightly before letting go. Abby snuck a little kiss, her lips tasted salty from the tears and then she pulled her up out of the bed. "Come on, put your clothes on, you can borrow some pyjama bottoms."

Broken

School resumed after the glorious rest and relaxation of the winter holiday with people feeling a little downhearted, for most, it was difficult just to get back into the routine of studying. The wet windy weather didn't help the dejected moods and for the girls, the sly digs from Tanya and her friends were particularly grating.

It seemed nothing had changed, she had not been punished for Lucia's fall or for publicly insulting Jo and if anything it had emboldened Tanya. It seemed that every day she got a little nastier, louder and more public.

Anne was still secretly recording these insults and had a collection of little video files on her PC at home. There were none which were particularly bad or incriminating though so she just let them accrue.

The girls were all envious of Susan and Jo's flat, though apparently Rick had spoken to Anne's dad and he was keeping an eye out for a flat in the same building. Since they had not even gotten conditional offers from the universities though, he had not been overly hasty.

In private Susan had joked that Abby and Anne could have the second bedroom in their flat but that had received a flat no from Rick who was quite insistent the girls keep separate bedrooms.

"I guess the rules would be the same if it was a boy I was going out with." Susan had rationalised when she was alone with Jo. "And of course, what they can't see won't hurt them!"

In the first week back Anne's guidance teacher had asked her "Why didn't you apply to better universities? With your grades, you could get into somewhere with a far better reputation."

Apparently her reply of, "I would prefer to have friends who can support and motivate me." was incorrect. At least that was her assumption after the long lecture she received.

"You know, I'm pretty sure I would hate being alone in a new school." she kicked the ground, "At least Lucia has had Mae to keep her company." They were walking slowly between classes, "Anyway, who cares about reputation!"

Suddenly Tanya pushed past them, jostling them into each other, "Yeah losers, it's not like your reputation isn't mud already." then she was gone.

"What the fuck! She's listening to our conversations now?" Abby complained, "How fucking long has she been there?"

Anne looked around carefully, "We can check tonight." She whispered, "Want to come round and check after school?"

"Sure, but what did the teacher mean 'why didn't you apply'? Surely you applied for other universities?" Abby stopped walking when she didn't get a reply. "Anne?"

"I only applied for one university." Anne said, speaking to the ground.

"But why? Surely you need a backup? What if you don't get in?" Abby asked in disbelief.

"I decided I don't want to go anywhere else. If I don't get in, I'll do another year." She mumbled.

"Anne... why?"

"I'm following you. If you take a different uni I'll apply there. I can take a gap year, work in whichever city. Something. I don't want to lose you." She said in a small voice.

Abby just gathered her in her arms, "Well, I guess we all just have to get good grades and get our preferred placements!" She squeezed her tight. "Okay?"

Anne nodded. "Good. Now, quickly, let's get to class." Abby said, pulling her along.

For the next few weeks, the teachers worked them hard, revising the work done the term before whilst also ploughing on with new work. It was stressful and worrying. They all knew the teachers were privy to some of the exam results before they got released and everyone assumed they were revising the bits people got wrong.

"Geeze I am so looking forward to music." Jo stated, standing in their customary indoor corner. "It's pretty much the only subject that isn't ridiculous just now."

"I thought you did PE?" Heather asked.

"Yeah, and they have us in an old classroom studying anatomy! I swear that the classroom hasn't been used since the sixties. I think they filmed To Sir With Love in it! It's so old and musty that it's got a blackboard instead of a whiteboard!"

"How un-PC of them!" Abby laughed. "Actually, perhaps it's the opposite, we should have a rally defending the rights of the poor downtrodden blackboards that are out of work!"

"Oh shut up!" Jo said, joining in Abby laughter.

"Hey, To Sir With Love was a classic, and I think my mum has a copy. Cool, I needed a new film for the hat on film night!" Heather said, dragging a pen and jotter from her bag.

"Oh god, that film was so slow." Anne complained. "I hate to say but I'm hoping no one draws that one out."

"I've never watched it, the song was nice though. What's it about?" Jo asked.

"Erm, race relations in the sixties? Mutual respect, something like that." Anne answered somewhat unsure. "It's been a few years since we watched it."

Later that day Jo and Abby were outside in the courtyard, again waiting for the rest of their friends. The day had brightened and it was a balmy double digits outside so they had decided to make the most of it.

Abby used her sleeve to dry off the top of the wall and sat down. "Hey, Jo. Can I ask for some advice?"

Jo frowned and said "Sure!"

"Oh god, how do I start this... Remember last time we talked here and I said you wouldn't hear the story from me?"

Jo smiled, "Ye-es?"

"Well, I think I need to tell you the story."

Jo wiped the water off the wall beside Abby and sat down. "Go on, I'm listening."

"So, that day that you gave Anne advice, she came back to my place. She sort of explained everything and how she thought she might be a lesbian yeah?"

"Yeah." Jo said patiently.

"Well, I sort of did totally the wrong thing and suggested we just have sex right?"

"Okay...?"

"Yeah well, I said we could do this mutual masturbation thing and it could be under the covers and she could look me in the eyes and I thought it would be hot." Abby explained quickly before she could lose her nerve.

"Oooo! Saucy, I'm guessing by the fact you said she hadn't last time that she didn't go for it?"

"No, she erm... fled my room crying." Abby said in shame. "She thought I was being flippant or teasing her or something."

"Okay, but you made up and everything's good, yeah?" Jo asked with a frown, "Why tell me now?"

"Well, remember the other day when we made the snowman?"

"Oh god. The song! It was torture!" Jo said, putting her head in her hands. "Yeah?" she sighed.

"Well, we went home early. And my parents weren't home."

Jo looked at her wide-eyed. "And you guys... ? Really?" she asked with a big smile.

"Well, no..." Abby sighed, "We started to but... Anne really didn't erm... get off... " she trailed off, unsure how to continue.

Jo nodded, thinking. "Okay, well... shit." They sat in silence for a while before Jo spoke. "You know, some people are what's called asexual. It's kind of like, they aren't interested in sex, it isn't what makes them tick. Some of them don't get relationships either, like they don't feel romantic love at all."

She shuffled around so that she was sitting cross-legged, facing Abby and asked. "She likes kissing?" at Abby's nod she asked, "And she gets animated and... oh god this is embarrassing... you know... she gets into it?"

"Yeah, she was making all the right sounds and her hands were... yes, she seemed to enjoy it." Abby admitted.

"Well, you might be lucky, some people only get off on other people's erm... passion." Jo explained. "Or they don't get off at all but really enjoy the act." Abby was looking a little sad. "Hey, cheer up. You have a beautiful girlfriend who loves you and makes you happy. If she doesn't like sex... that's what vibrators were made for!"

Abby gave a little smile, "And you would know all about vibrators?"

"Hey, don't knock it till you try it. But honestly, just try going all the way with her, make sure not to focus entirely on her, like, don't expect her to enjoy it when you focus entirely on her pleasure. Don't obsess on the big O. See where it goes." she batted her friend on the shoulder, "And failing that, I can give you a website that sends things out in plain cardboard boxes!"

Abby laughed at that and they sat in companionable silence until the other girls showed up.

ele

"Hey, I heard they are handing out the results today!" Heather announced to her friends. "Want to not read them until after school? We can all go to the coffee shop and open them together!"

There was some grumbling, the idea had merit but the girls were itching to look at their score.

"Oh come on! It'll be great!" she pushed.

Eventually, everyone reluctantly agreed.

"What if everyone gets good grades and I tanked?" Susan asked, "It's going to suck!"

Jo gave her a hug, "Hey, you won't have. I think we all did well, and if not, we're all friends and we'll support you. Hell, if anyone needs help it might be a good thing that we know, we can help each other."

There were encouraging remarks from everyone, people were actually really keen on starting a study group after school, meeting at each other's houses.

"Erm, well, cool! I think. Perhaps we can start a Friday thing? Want to come around my house this week?" Heather asked, organising things on the fly, "We could go on the bus after school and get fish and chips for dinner?"

Everyone was keen.

The results were handed out at registration, making the delay in looking at them so much more frustrating. Every break when the girls met up people wanted to open them early. Heather insisted they wait, somehow making the girls listen to her.

The day dragged, every subject seemed to last an entire day. The other students were all happily discussing their results in class, lamenting the hard exams and celebrating their good grades. The teachers were going over parts of the exams that people found hard, it all made the wait so damned difficult!

Eventually, though the final bell rang and the girls all raced to meet at the back gate. This time there were only seconds between each of them arriving. To everyone but Jo's surprise, a few boys turned up too, including Brian who made sure to apologise to Susan for his previous behaviour when she met him here.

They headed down the road, excitedly chatting, the boys hadn't opened their results either, though somehow this didn't seem to bother them as much.

"You know, I doubt my dad would like me bringing boys home, even for a study group." Anne said, concerned they may feel left out.

"My parents won't care as long as they're in and we stick to the kitchen and living room." Heather said, "You're free to join when it's my turn." She seemed to mainly be talking to Brian.

When they reached the coffee shop they had to pull three tables together to accommodate everyone. The woman behind the counter seemed pretty pleased though, probably happy to have the custom.

They all ordered at the counter and paid, most of them also getting cream buns and sweet slices too.

"Right!" Heather called, taking charge again since it was her idea. "I think we do this by alphabetical order, first names only!"

"Aww! That means I'm first!" Abby complained.

"Votes for?" Heather called, almost every hand went up. "Motion carried! Abby, you're up!" She seemed to be enjoying her chairperson role.

Abby huffed and pulled the crumpled white envelope from her bag. She nervously tore it open, face scrunched up in anticipation. Anne gave her a one-armed hug.

"Erm... not bad... enough for the uni entrance I think." She handed the paper to Anne and it then got passed around the table. "I guess I just need to work on English."

"Right, my turn." Anne said, giving Abby's hand a quick squeeze. She tore the envelope open and looked at the paper. "Hmmm, yep." Was all she said before passing it to Abby.

"Holy crap! Your results are insane! Anne, you could have gotten into fucking medicine in any fucking university in the country." She passed the sheet to the right. "Fuck." She said, dropping her head into her hands. She had a sinking feeling that she was ruining her friends future by letting her follow her to a sub-par uni.

"Hey, you can't compare yourself to Anne! Come on Brian, your turn, show her a normal score." Heather said, misunderstanding Abby's despair.

Brian's results were fairly bad, he hadn't expected much though. They all got pretty much exactly the scores they expected until it came to Jo.

"Holy fuck!" She exclaimed, dropping the paper and putting her hand over her mouth.

"What?" Heather exclaimed, reaching over and grabbing the paper. "Jo, these are great, what's wrong?"

Jo blinked, "Erm, I've never gotten grades that good. I... I think I'm going to university!" She blinked back tears. "Holy shit. I have to phone my mum... and Jenny's mum too!" She pushed her chair back and went outside, already dialling the number.

Susan watched her go, smiling wistfully.

"Right, well! Kevin, your turn." Heather took control again.

———ele———

Jo returned just in time to hear Susan's result, which wasn't bad, certainly enough for the entry requirement on the business studies course she wanted to enrol in. She gave her a big hug, "What did your mum say?" She asked, enjoying the huge smile on her girlfriend's face.

"She's stoked, she wanted us to go out for dinner but I don't think she's up for that. What did I miss?" Jo asked.

"Well, turn's out Kevin is a math's whizz but pretty crap at everything else." This got a protest from Kevin. "And Michael isn't bad at physics." She gave the boy in question a nod and thumbs up. "Hey, perhaps my mum might like to have you guys around again? She really enjoyed Christmas. Perhaps you can stay the night again?"

"Mmm, I liked that." Jo agreed.

"So, study groups!" Heather called after the last results had been read out. "Who wants to come round on Friday?" There was a show of hands, unsurprisingly including most of the boys. "Hmm, right, might be a tight fit. Okay, who needs maths and sciences?" She took a note, "and who needs English, languages and the soggy subjects?" It was obvious her views on the 'humanities' subjects. "Okay, we need some crossover, people good at the subjects to tutor. How about we have the sciences at my place this week and the rest at someone else's next week?" Seeing everyone's agreement she asked "Anne, would you be okay coming to tutor?"

Since her girlfriend would be there she readily agreed.

———ℓℓ———

Jo was excited for the rogaine season starting up, she always loved the orienteering events because she got to see trails and places she never knew existed. The maps for the rogaine events were utterly different to anything else, they had trails marked that sometimes you could pass three times looking for the intersection before you found it. The map points were often in places you wouldn't visit on a run and the event felt like an adventure.

She had been doing the local rogaine runs for years and still, the organisers managed to pick new areas to run courses on. The first one this season was brand new, Jo had run some of the trails but it wasn't exactly her stomping ground. Susan was going to join her on one of the later ones, once it was less dark at night, she wasn't overly fond of downhill running in the dark yet. This event Jo was doing alone. She was planning on pushing hard, going to the furthest out points first, they normally scored the highest points. She was feeling fast just now, strong, she was going to do well.

She packed her small camelback bag with the required gear, gloves, hat, emergency blanket, windproof jacket, first aid kit, water and food and of course her new compass. She also packed a spare battery for her head torch, fresh socks, some homemade energy gels and some boiled sweets. She slipped her phone in the back and fitted her new GoPro to the backpack strap.

She was wearing her good thermals and her high vis woolly hat so she wouldn't be cold. Susan's mum had bought her new shoes for her birthday too and they were only just worn in.

Her dad was going to drop her at the starting point on his way to work and she always got a lift home from the organiser. She looked again and realised she had forgotten a pen, she grabbed her favourite one, the one she kept for special occasions, Susan's purple gel pen. She smiled recalling her girlfriend giving it to her, it definitely brought her good luck.

She got in the car with her dad and realised he was listening to her CD, it gave her a little warm feeling in her chest. They didn't say much on the way to the start point, it was a rural one, she far preferred the courses in the countryside to the urban ones but it did mean her dad had to drive a long way out of his normal route to take her. She knew he didn't mind but she still felt bad.

"Okay dad, have fun at work. I'll text you to tell you I'm home safe." She said, getting out of the car.

"Here, take this just in case." He said, handing her a twenty. "You never know."

She smiled at him and put it into her backpack, "I'll give you it back tomorrow. But thanks."

She watched him drive off before turning to the registration table which had been set up behind the organiser's car. "So, is there going to be less gorse than the last one?" she asked cheekily.

"Nope, if anything more." her friend replied. "It builds character."

She laughed and gave the old man her entry fee, receiving a map, a code sheet and a plastic zip-lock bag in return.

"So, any hints?" She asked, peering at the map and working out her planned route.

"Yep, run fast, find lots of map points, write the numbers down." He said gruffly. He had never given her any other advice, it was almost a mantra now.

She laughed, "Good advice old man. Many people show up yet?"

"Nah, you're pretty early. Want a biscuit?" He asked, offering her a pack of digestives.

"Sure, budge up." She answered, sitting down beside him in the boot of his car.

She helped him hand out the maps for a while, passing the time before the start.

"You'd best warm-up." He said to her, she had lost track of time and there were only a few minutes until the start.

Whilst she was stretching and warming up her friend did the pre-race brief, "Right, most of you, if not all, have heard this numerous times but listen up anyway. Time starts when I blow the whistle, it stops in three hours. If you are late, points will be deducted for each minute past the time. If you know you will be late and are not in trouble, call the number on the code sheet, if you are later than thirty minutes and have not called me, I will call you, if you do not answer, we will send out search and rescue." He waited to let this sink in. "Do NOT make me send out a search party if you got cold and went home!"

"Now, scores are marked on the code sheet, if you get to a map point and cannot find the code on the shiny piece of fabric, take a photo of the location, if many people are unable to find that code we may still award the points. Take care and have fun!"

He blew the whistle and everyone scattered, some walkers heading to nearby points, some runners going clockwise, some anticlockwise. Jo headed with the people going anticlockwise as she knew the steepest bit would then be downhill.

She overtook many of the slower runners within the first few hundred meters and then kept pace with a group who were travelling at a decent pace. There were a few map points they passed at the beginning but they were only worth ten points, she had no plans to stop until the first fifty points one and then if she had time at the end she would grab as many of the local tens and twenties that she could.

When the group eventually reached the first point it wasn't obvious, the group she was behind milled about looking whilst she looked at the map. She worked out the point was actually off the track and about fifty metres up the hill, noticing a tiny side trail she followed it and found the marker. She wrote the four-letter code on her sheet in her nice purple pen and took off, making a good distance on the group she had been following.

She looked at the map as she ran, using her compass to determine her location relative to the next point. It looked like it was up a stream bed to the right of the track so she figured she would see the stream easily.

With her next attack point in mind, she pushed on faster, hoping to get further Infront of the pack.

Right enough, a couple of kilometres in she heard the stream and after getting her feet wet wading she easily found the next marker. She was already a hundred points up and was only a half-hour in, the next four codes were worth a hundred each.

She knew from the sheet that there were one thousand seven hundred points in total and there had been groups that almost got that number last year so, with that in mind she pushed on even harder.

By the time she reached the furthest marker she was fairly exhausted, she took a breather to have a drink and one of her energy gels. After catching her breath she checked the map again, marking some good geographical features as attack points and pushed on downhill.

It was downhill she loved, pushing at a breakneck pace, trusting in your shoes and gravity to keep you upright at the edge of control. Her head torch lit the trail in a circle, outside of which was pitch black. She was hoping the footage from the GoPro would come out well, she hadn't tried it in the dark yet.

She passed a single runner coming the other way and waved, he was panting so hard that he couldn't talk and they were both going so fast that he was gone in a fraction of a second.

She rounded a bend and came across the first of her attack points, a cliff dropping off on the right-hand side of the trail, so she slowed down, not wanting to miss the next feature.

Just as she slowed, a figure in dark clothing lept from the shadows with a scream of "Die bitch!" Jo however was quick on her feet and had really good reaction times, she spun out of the way of the arms reaching to shove her and skidded to a halt a few meters down the track.

She turned around and there was no sign of anyone on the track. She looked around, her posture defensive and ready for a fight but there was no one there. Confused, she warily looked over the edge of the cliff. There was no obvious sign that anyone had fallen, her head torch only illuminating the closest foliage at the bottom of the rocky cliff.

"Shit." She said out loud. She backed away from the edge and looked up the hill, wondering if her assailant had fled upwards.

"Fuck it." She eventually said and pulled her phone from the depths of her backpack.

She dialled the organiser's number and her friend answered on the first ring, "Jo, everything okay?" He asked, obviously having her number in his contacts.

"Erm, something weird just happened. Someone just jumped out at me and then disappeared. I don't know if they ran off or if they fell down the hill but by the time I turned around they were gone." Jo explained. "I don't know whether I should be calling the police or mountain rescue or if I should just ignore it. What should I do Abe?"

The old man thought for a minute, "Well, they didn't go past you? Is there anyone likely to be behind you?"

"Yeah, there was a group I passed a ways back, probably a few minutes out." Jo replied.

"Okay, where are you?"

Jo looked at her map and estimated her position, then read out the map reference and said, "I can give you the GPS location once I'm off the phone."

"Okay, wait for the next group to come and call me back. I'm going to tee up the mountain rescue guys."

Joe hung up and sat down on the side of the trail. "Well shit. I guess I'm not winning this one." She said sadly.

It took a few long minutes before the group she had passed arrived. They stopped, thinking she may have hurt herself considering she was sitting down.

"Did you pass anyone on the way down? Someone dressed in black?" She asked them.

They hadn't passed anyone but the runner Jo had seen up the top.

"Damn, they probably fell in that case. Okay, I'm calling Abe to get search and rescue." She picked up the phone, "You know, you guys may as well continue, no point all of us dropping out" she said before making the call.

The runners discussed this whilst Jo was on the phone.

"We're going down the hill to see if we can find them, Lisa is going to stay and keep you company." One of the men said, "The sooner we find her the better the outcome is likely to be, even if it's just directing the rescue team."

"Sounds good. Thanks." Jo replied.

Jo then called her mum and explained before calling her girlfriend.

"Yeah, it might have been Tanya. I don't know, it all happened so fast, I didn't see anything really. Hopefully, it's on the GoPro. Yeah, love you too." She finished the call and sat back with the other runner waiting for help to arrive.

"So, you think you may have known this girl?" The woman asked her.

"Yeah, she's been terrorising my friends all year. We're pretty sure she pushed one of them down a flight of stairs."

"Well, I must say I'm impressed you even called the emergency services. I'm sure it would have been tempting to just leave her." The woman suggested.

"Yeah, I guess, I never really even considered it."

They sat in companionable silence, waving at passing runners and occasionally explaining the situation until someone called Jo's phone.

"Abe! Did they find her?" She asked.

"Yeah, they're showing the rescue guys where she is just now. You can come back now, we don't need you to wait up there." Abe told her.

ele

They left off at a fast run, the woman, Lisa, leading the way. Seeing that Jo was easily keeping up she sped up, and kept speeding up until they were both at breakneck speed. They stayed running flat out until they reached the car park where the finish point was, whooping and high diving each other as they stopped, panting by Abe's car.

"The police want to see you Jo, that girl they pulled out says you pushed her." Abe said, returning from the Ambulance sitting a little way off with its lights dark. "They're going to be another hour before they get the girl out. The place she landed is pretty far off the track and she's strapped to a stretcher in case her back's broken. You'd better give them your side of the story before she gets here."

"Oh man, I swear she's a nutcase!" Jo said, walking towards the police officers at the other side of the car park.

"Hey, I'm Jo." She introduced herself, unhooking her GoPro from her bag strap. "Look, I know she's telling you some bullshit about me pushing her but hopefully the footage on my camera will back me up." She handed the camera to the policewoman, "Honestly, I think she was trying to kill me up there, we're pretty sure she pushed my friend Lucia down the stairs at school and she's been verbally harassing us for months."

The policewoman took the camera and placed it in an evidence bag. "Okay, come over here and we can take your statement." She led Jo away to the police car where Jo gave her as much detail as she could.

"Okay, you say she's been harassing yourself and your friends. Can people corroborate your story?" The officer asked.

"Oh, we have some footage of her attacking us at the ice rink, and my friend has some clips of her abusing us in the corridors. The guy in the ice rink would back us up, and we reported her to the school a few times." Jo said, not sure what else they could want.

"Hey, that's great, can you get your friend to bring in the footage? And we can talk with the guy at the ice rink, do you remember his name?"

"Erm, no but he was the manager, a huge dude, you know, man-mountain sort of thing."

The officer smiled at the description and wrote it down. "Okay, I have your details. There's no point in keeping you so you can go home when you're ready."

"Okay, I'm getting a lift with Abe, the organiser so I need to stay till the end. Anyway, I don't want to miss the pizza!" She got up to leave.

"Oh, here's my card so that you can contact me. You've had quite a night, so make sure you talk to someone, and if you need to you can call me, even if it's just to chat about what happened." The policewoman said, handing her the card.

Jo thanked her and headed over to Abe.

"You know, Lisa here says she can take you home if you like." Abe said as she approached. "We still have an hour till the race ends and another half till I can leave."

"Not to be crass but, I'm really hungry, I was looking forward to the pizza!" Jo admitted. "Not so much looking forward to seeing them carrying out the cray cray though!" Her slang for crazy amused Abe.

"Hey, I'm hungry too, how about I buy us pizza and we eat it at your house? We can talk to your mum on the way?" Lisa asked.

Jo thought about this for a bit, she didn't know the woman but Abe seemed to. Eventually realising she was quite cold and shaky she relented, "Yeah, I can call mum and Susan on the way. Thanks."

They picked up enough pizza to share with Jo's mum and Susan, it turned out her girlfriend had gotten her dad to drop her round when she heard about the attack.

They arrived at the flat and Lisa was really helpful, fielding questions from Susan and Jo's mum whilst Jo tucked into the pizza. She found that even after eating her fill and warming up, going so far as to change clothes, she was still shaking.

"Jo, you did well today, it's okay to be shaken when someone tries to kill you! You did everything right so you have nothing to worry about. Okay?" Lisa assured her as she made her way to the door. "I would have a hot shower and go to bed. It will all seem better tomorrow."

She said her goodbyes and left. Then Jo realised Susan had no way of getting home.

"Is your dad going to collect you?" She asked, coming back to the kitchen table.

"Your mum said I could stay the night." Susan explained.

"Oh, I should change the sheets!" Jo said with panic in her eyes, it would be the first time Susan had stayed at their house.

"I did it already Jo." Her mum said.

"Mum! You're not meant to be doing things like that!" Jo complained.

"Hey, I'm no invalid! Now, you and Susan go shower before bed. No hanky panky!"

It was dawning on Susan that Jo's mum might be daft.

They stood in the shower, Jo's body was actually cold to the touch, and she was shaking. Susan just held her, standing under the shower until the hot water ran out. It turned out she possibly wasn't daft at all.

_ℓℓ_

The next day they took a trip to Anne's house. The whole family was there for the explanation, Kelly was adamant she would have left Tanya to die, Pete felt he may have done the same.

"You did the right thing," Jane assured her, "the girl belongs in a white room with padded walls but letting her die would have weighed on your conscience like a brick."

"I'm just glad I had my new GoPro, she was telling everyone I pushed her! I really hope the footage comes out okay."Jo said, "The police asked me to get you to bring in the clips of her insulting us and the stuff from the ice rink. I was hoping you might be able to do that today to get it out the way?"

"Sure, we can go right after we finish our coffee. Anne, can you nip and copy it onto a USB stick?" Pete asked, pouring the girls another coffee.

"Thanks Pete." Susan said, accepting the refill. "I'm glad we have all this proof, I would hate for her to put this all on Jo. God, it would have ruined her chances with the scholarship."

"Yeah, at the time I just did it to placate Anne and get her to go back to school, I wasn't even convinced it was Tanya! To be honest I expected this to all blow over after that one incident."

Pete took the girls to the police station with the promise of bowling afterwards, of course, Kelly had invited herself and Anne had insisted on Abby coming so they were in what he called the mummy mobile for the extra seats. His wife of course called it her urban assault vehicle.

"So, you guys are sure you're okay bussing home after the bowling?" He asked, concerned that Jo had just had a traumatic experience.

"Yes dad. It's fine, we take the bus every day!" Anne insisted.

"And this isn't an excuse for you to meet up with boys?" Susan made a tiny sputtering noise trying to keep her laughed in.

"Well, obviously not you two. I trust you for one thing." He eyed Abby in the rearview mirror, "Not so much the others, especially with Abby egging them on." He was only half-joking.

Susan smiled at her friends, enjoying the inside joke.

"Yep, can't trust me with your daughters, I'm a corrupting influence!" Abby said proudly.

Pete only answered with a "Hmm" as he pulled into the police car park.

Surprisingly the officers from the previous night had just started their shift but they had to wait about ten minutes before they could see them, probably putting on uniforms and arranging paperwork and rooms.

"Hi," the officer started as she came through the door before noticing the crowd. "Oh, erm, you brought back up!" She laughed. "Well, if you don't mind them all being privy to the information we can probably all fit in the interview room as long as people don't mind standing. I have a laptop to get that footage from you."

She ushered them through into a small room with four chairs and a table. Anne and Jo sat down opposite the two police officers and the others stood behind them, Pete with a hand on Anne's shoulder in support.

"Okay, so I would like to start by showing you the footage from last night. It's actually really good, it shows exactly what happened." She turned her laptop around and pressed play.

The clip started a little way up the trail and you saw Jo's hands holding a compass and map pumping in rhythm. The head torch lit the scene well and as she came to the corner you clearly heard a voice cry 'Die bitch!' as a figure entered the camera's vision. The footage panned and shifted wildly and you could hear Jo's shoes skid on the gravel.

"Now, we watched from the beginning so we know you didn't plan an ambush or any such nonsense, we slowed down the video." At this point, she turned the laptop and brought up some still pictures. "You can make out the assailant's face here, and on this next one you see a flash of her falling as you turn back." There was a vague black shape and what could have been a hand.

"Anyway, we are happy that your version of events is correct. That being the case the assailant has changed her testimony." She took Anne's USB stick as she was talking. "I doubt you will like her new tack."

She started the files copying over before giving Jo her full attention. "She now claims she has been in love with you for years and seeing you with your new girlfriend caused her to snap."

"Oh for fuck sake!" Jo exclaimed, "Sorry. Sorry. Man that girl is a manipulative cow. What does she think is going to happen with that bullshit?"

"I shouldn't really comment but she's probably going for some psychiatric plea. Even though she is a few months off her eighteenth birthday and so will be tried as a juvenile, attempted murder is a very serious offence. She is likely looking at jail time." The officer explained.

They waited as they checked the footage off Anne's camera. "Now, we are not meant to encourage people using hidden cameras but this certainly does show that she was engaged in a prolonged harassment of you and your friends." She handed the USB stick back and fished Jo's camera from her pocket. "We don't need to keep these, the digital footage is enough. Thank you for coming in. We'll be in touch as the case progresses." She stood and made to let them out.

They filed out the door but as Jo was leaving she turned and asked "Before I go, how badly was she hurt? Will she recover?"

"She was quite lucky, broke both her legs, her pelvis and one of her lower vertebrae but they don't think she damaged her spinal column

so she should be fine, eventually. She will be in traction for a while."
The male offer replied.

"Good." Jo nodded and left the room.

When they reached the outside world Jo released a shuddering breath.
"It's over. She's gone. Oh geez, what a relief. I don't think I realised
how stressful having her torment us was." She closed her eyes and
took a few deep breaths turning her head to the sky. "Woo!" She
whooped into the air, a huge smile coming onto her face. "Let's go
bowling! Susan can show you how much she's improved. I suspect
she's going to whoop your asses."

Inclusion

The incident with Tanya weighed on Jo's mind, even after the police had told her she wasn't returning to school, that she wouldn't have to give evidence at a trial, would never have to see the girl again, still she couldn't stop the incident going around in her head. It kept her up at night.

Halfway through the week she visited the police station again, voluntarily and without telling anyone. She waited nervously at the front desk biting her nails and tapping her heels. The arresting officer had been busy and she waited twenty minutes in the hard plastic orange seat staring at the notice board, re-reading the crime stoppers posters over and over.

"Jo, I didn't expect to see you again." It was the male officer, she hadn't spoken much to him and it didn't help her confidence.

Jo got up and shook the man's hand, "Hi, I erm... wondered whether I could see Tanya?"

The man smiled and nodded, "Interestingly we often get people asking to speak to their attackers. Generally, we don't recommend it. Often it will harm the case against the person and often it wont give the satisfactory outcome people expect."

Jo closed her eyes and sighed, "I thought you might say that. I just wanted to ask her why." She took a deep breath and looked up at the police officer. "Thank you for your time." She said, shaking his hand and turning to leave.

"She is still in hospital by the way. She won't go into custody until she has healed up." The officer mentioned in what appeared to Jo a purposefully offhand manner.

Jo paused half way out of the door, "Thanks." She said, giving him a nod and a small smile.

As she slowly descended the steps outside the police station she pondered whether she should risk a visit to the hospital. She looked to the sky, almost tempted to ask for guidance. "Fuck it." She said out loud and set off at an easy jog towards the hospital.

It was a twenty minute jog to the hospital, thoughts of what she wanted to say whirred through Jo's head the whole way, along with the occasional doubt that she was doing the wrong thing. She hadn't even worked up a sweat by the time she got there, her heart rate actually went up as she approached the front desk as her nervousness increased.

"Hi, I was wondering which ward Tanya Goldwin was in?" She asked the nurse behind the front desk.

The nurse narrowed her eyes and her brow furrowed, "I assume you aren't family?" She asked in a sharp tone. "The police have asked that we not allow her friends to visit."

"Oh, I'm certainly not a friend. It was me she was trying to push off a cliff." Jo replied, enjoying the look of surprise on the nurse's face.

"Well, I'm doubly unsure I should let you see her now." The nurse looked Jo up and down and huffed. "Hold on."

She went out the back to speak with an elderly woman, Jo couldn't hear the hushed conversation but they both snuck glanced back towards her more than once.

The elderly nurse shuffled out and gave Jo a thorough appraising look. "You aren't here to cause trouble?" She asked with a voice that sounded like she had smoked a pack a day since she was a small child.

"I just wanted to ask her why she attacked myself and my friends. It just doesn't make a lot of sense to me." Jo responded quietly.

"Hmm." The woman huffed, dismissively. "From what I have seen of her she is just a repulsive child." She levered the folding desk with great effort and stepped out to the foyer. "Come on. I'm not leaving you two alone." She said gruffly and shuffled off towards the lift.

They stood in the lift silently, Jo trying to ignore the stale smoke smell which was cloying in such a small space. She felt glad, not for the first time, that she had stopped smoking.

The lift stopped with a jerk, the doors sliding open to reveal another busy foyer, hallways stretching off on both sides of the desk. The woman hobbled over to the desk and grabbed a clipboard, "Sign your name on this. All her visitors have to be registered."

Jo took the board and carefully wrote her name and who she was visiting before signing. She noted that there were very few other names and they all had the surname of Goldwin.

"Right, just so you know, this isn't going to be a long visit. I have things to do." The nurse told her as she handed the clipboard back.

They walked down the left hand corridor all the way to the end, the nurse was huffing after the short distance and looked like her hips were giving her issues. "Don't get old." She said as she saw Jo looking at her.

"Oi, missy." The nurse called loudly as they entered the room, waking Tanya. "You've got a visitor."

Tanya looked blearily towards Jo and then when she worked out who it was shouted, "Fuck off." in a slurred voice.

"You be polite for once in your life." The nurse told her sharply, sitting down in the corner chair, "We aren't leaving until you give this poor girl some answers."

"I don't have to." Tanya said, again sounding like she had been to the dentist.

"Well, I control your pain medication and if you don't then I might just decide you are on too high a dosage young girl." The nurse counters.

Tanya huffed and threw her head back on the pillow. Her body was in a full cast with both her legs elevated. "Fuck you all." She said in a defeated tone.

Jo walked slowly over to the bed and sat in the chair. She stared at the girl in the bed, neither one speaking, Tanya resolutely staring at the ceiling.

"Why?" She asked eventually.

There was no response from Tanya.

"We did nothing to you. I don't think any one of us had spoken more than a few words to you before you started harassing us." She waited for a response which never came.

"Lucia isn't even gay. You pushed her down the stairs for what? For being my friend?" She watched Tanya's face, trying to read the emotions flickering past.

"And that excuse you gave to the police? That you are in love with me? I know we have never once spoken before this year and even now, not one civil conversation." She watched a tear leak from the corner of Tanya's eye.

"Are you crying for yourself? Is it remorse for what you tried to do? You tried to kill me Tanya, surely you can tell me why you would want to do that?"

Tanya turned her head at last, "Eve was my friend." She turned back to stare at the roof, as if that answered everything.

"Eve, my ex-girlfriend? Eve, who wouldn't even see me after I came out? Eve, who moved school to get away from me?" Jo shook her head, "What exactly can you mean by that?"

"She killed herself." Tanya said, speaking to the ceiling, tears freely running down towards her hair. "She was my best friend and she killed herself." She turned to look at Jo again, "She killed herself because of you."

"What?" Jo asked, shocked at the revelation and bemused at the accusation. "How can it be my fault?"

"Her parents sent her to a camp to 'fix' her. Before she met you. Conversion therapy or something. As soon as her parents heard that she had a gay friend they made her move schools again."

"So it's my fault she moved schools? And what? She couldn't live without me?" Jo asked incredulously.

"No, she got sent to another camp. She killed herself there. I think she couldn't bear to not be herself." She was mumbling, still slightly slurring her words. "But 's your fault she got sent there."

"So, why not attack me? Why my friends? And why not straight after Eve died, that must have been a couple of years ago?" Jo asked, still not understanding.

"You had no friends. Thought it was a good punishment. I tried to drive your new friends away." she trailed off, her eyes closed. "Then I figured it wasn't enough." Her eyes scrunched up, more tears being pushed out of the corners, "I miss her so much."

"That's the thing though, I miss her too." Jo said, a tear running down her own cheek.

The next day the group were approached by Tanya's group, it was exceedingly intimidating, especially because there were more girls than they had seen with Tanya in some time, and a number of boys.

A girl who seemed to be the appointed negotiator for the group stepped forward, "We heard about Tanya." She started, then stopped obviously unsure how to continue.

Jo stepped in front of her friends, presenting her normal tough image. "Yeah?"

"Well, we just wanted to say... erm, we thought before that Tanya hadn't pushed your friend down the stairs. She told us you were just trying to get her in trouble... erm..." she looked back at the huge group, looking for encouragement. "Yeah, so, after last night... we believe you, some of us stayed with her." She gave a girl in the back a dirty look, "But we realise now that Tanya was just bullying you and we, or at least some of us, went along with her. We enabled her behaviour." This part was obviously coming from a parent or a teacher. "And we want to apologise. We truly are not anti-gay or anything and erm... We feel really bad for letting her bully you all this time." The girl finished and there were sheepish looks from the crowd.

One of the boys stepped forward, "We are sorry. Please, if anyone says anything to you from now on, tell us, we'll support you."

Jo frowned, "You boys didn't do anything though."

"We knew about it and didn't speak up. That's just as bad." There was some agreement from behind him.

Jo glanced at her friends. "Well, I guess we accept your apology. As long as they aren't empty words and things do change then well, we bear you no ill will and it's water under the bridge. Just, you know, attacking people because of their sexuality is really not cool."

She stepped forward and held out her hand, "A new start?"

The boy shook her hand and said, "Yeah, new start. Thank you."

The crowd disbursed and Jo breathed a sigh of relief. "Holy shit that was scary. I swear my knees are weak." Her girlfriend hugged her.

"Thanks for dealing with that Jo, I was bricking it." Heather admitted, "If you hadn't been here I think I might have just run away."

"Hey, that's a story for one of those interview questions we had to practice in guidance class! You know 'tell us of a time you dealt with a high-stress situation'" Abby suggested, "I had nothing for that one last week!"

—ℓℓ—

The girls began to relax, starting to feel safe at school for the first time since the beginning of the school year.

"Abby, I think I'm ready to tell them." Anne whispered.

"What now?" Abby asked.

"Just our friends, Heather and Mae and Jenny, maybe the boys. Not mum and dad, or you know, the school. Not yet." Anne admitted.

"So, a 'soft' coming out, just to see how it goes?" Abby confirmed.

"Yeah. Then we can cuddle at film night on Saturday." Anne said coyly.

"Okay, guys!" Abby said loudly, getting everyone's attention before Anne could chicken out. "We have an announcement."

The group turned to face them, "Susan and Jo already know, but Anne and I have been seeing each other for about seven months now." She searched the amused faces. "What?" She asked.

"We've just been waiting for you to tell us." Jenny said, smiling cheekily.

Anne looked accusingly at Jo and Susan, "Hey, we didn't tell them. Honestly, not a word."

"It's been pretty obvious, the looks and the little touches. Honestly, we were starting to wonder if you guys knew! Mae was suggesting some kind of intervention." Heather joked.

Anne looked shocked, "Well, don't tell our parents, or the rest of the school. Perhaps the boys but not until the study group. And tell them it's kind of a secret."

"What's a secret?" Brian asked, walking up and snaking his arm around Heather.

"Anne and Abby are lesbians, but don't share it around." Heather told him.

"Fuck!" Brian exclaimed, "I owe Kevin a twenty."

"You bet on us being lesbians?" Abby hissed incredulously.

"Yeah well, I told Kevin to ask you out because he likes you, he said you were probably a lesbian because that would be just his luck and I bet him you weren't." He said bashfully, "I mainly did it to goad him into asking you." Susan slapped his leg, reproachfully.

"Why aren't you telling your parents?" Jenny asked.

"Because then they will never have any alone time!" Susan answered for them, "Honestly it feels like Jo and I are chaperoned every time we are together now!" She winked at her girlfriend, "I can't tell you how frustrating it is!"

"Ooh, sexy lesbian fun times? Don't tell the guys." Brian said, "Guaranteed they will ask for details."

"And you won't? Brian, are you growing up?" Jo teased.

"Nah, I just know you wouldn't tell me!" He admitted with a sly smile, earning him another slap on the leg.

"Are you sure your dad won't let you invite boys for movie night Anne? I'm starting to feel like the odd one out." Heather joked.

"Nope, in fact, I think if we come out, movie night might stop. Dad really doesn't trust Abby!" Anne replied.

"Oh god, I almost died in the car trying not to laugh when he said that!" Susan said giggling.

"Well, he wouldn't want to come this week anyway, it's dirty dancing." Abby reminded them, "Damned Kelly! I don't think she should have gotten a movie vote."

"Hey, don't knock Patrick Swayze, I understand why she chose it! Just because you don't swing that way." Heather teased. The four girls in the know shared a smile.

In a flurry of study and life, weeks and months passed and a new deadline for nerves came calling. The end of May was when conditional offers were handed out by the universities and then almost straight after they had exams. Everyone in the study group was convinced they would get better results in the real exams, even Anne swore that her top marks would be far higher. The boys had gone from scraping past in most of their classes to actually getting decent grades, and they were trying to stop smoking. They were mainly failing to stop but they had weeks where they would avoid smoking a single cigarette and overall they had cut down hugely. Jo was exceedingly proud of them.

"So, are we going to celebrate if we get offers? Or, I guess commiserate?" Heather asked. "By that time I will be eighteen, I can get us some wine or something."

"I don't drink." Jo said, "It plays hell with the training. Also, I like to feel in control."

"Okay, a big no from the only other legal drinker. What about the others?" She looked around.

"I'm staying sober if Jo is, I don't want to make a fool of myself." Susan decided.

Abby looked at Anne who shrugged, "We can't get too drunk, I assume we're doing this at movie night round Anne's house?" There was a nod of agreement. "Well, we have to sneak it in and we can't make a racket or anything." Again Heather agreed. "Well, maybe a glass or two. I think bubbles would be appropriate?"

Jenny was up for some alcohol and Heather assured them that Mae loved to drink so they gave Heather some money in advance. "We had better not get caught!"

The next two weeks flew past, the teachers were trying to cram so much knowledge into their students' heads that it was a wonder they didn't crack open. The Friday that the acceptances went online also marked a week-long optional study leave and the group had planned to use the mornings to come into school and utilise the teachers time for targeted revision and then meet up with their study group at people's houses for a group study.

First, however, was the acceptance postings, then movie night.

The girls all checked their acceptances before breakfast on the Friday, nothing had been posted. They then checked between classes the whole morning, nothing.

"Arg! Why! Why can't they just say they will post them at midday, or three or something. This waiting game sucks!" Heather fumed.

"I got one." Jenny said quietly. "Still waiting for the others but... I got into engineering down south."

"That's great!" Heather said, "Congratulations!" She went back onto the site and refreshed the page. Nothing.

By the end of the lunch break, however, Susan, Abby and Heather had at least one conditional offer, though not for their preferred local university.

"Grr!" Heather pantomimed throwing her phone. "Bloody stupid university! They better be more organized than this when it comes to our courses!"

The nerves were high going back to class after lunch, especially when all the other students were excitedly discussing their offers. The girls doggedly stuck to the revision, trying to ignore the situation. Trying to pretend they cared about titration or Russia under Lenin and Stalin and in Jo's case, the biomechanics of the knee joint.

Anne in particular was concentrating more on the coloured pens she was using to make her study notes than the content. She had placed all her eggs in one basket and now was panicking, Abby had been accepted at a different university. What if she wanted to go there? What if one of them didn't even get an offer from their preferred choice. She assumed she would get an offer. She had applied for five different courses at the same university, she had good grades and an unblemished school record. She was a model student. There was no reason for them not to want her. But what if they didn't want Abby? Her art was awesome, and her grades were... okay. Surely she would get in, but then, she only applied for one course. What if there was a huge contention for that course? What if the other applicants had better grades?

The what-ifs went around and around in her head. So much so that she was called out for being distracted, she looked down and realised that she had been drawing spirals and trees on her notes. "Sorry Sir, I'm a little distracted with the acceptance postings."

"Okay, come here, I want to have a chat with you." She nervously got out of her seat and followed him out of the classroom.

"Anne, you're my best student, bar none. Have you had a rejection? I may be able to help, give a recommendation or something?" He asked seriously.

"No! No, nothing like that. Just... haven't heard yet." she trailed off.

"Really? Not from any of the universities?" He asked in disbelief.

"I only applied for one." she said in a voice so quiet he could hardly hear.

"Okay, that's fine, you had your heart set on a specific institution. People do that. I'm sure you will be fine." He said, but stopped, seeing a look on her face. "It's not that is it?"

"No." she said sullenly.

"Okay, what then? Come on, I can't help if you don't tell me." He coaxed.

"I'm worried Abby might not come with me." She said quietly.

"Abby Rosenberg? Surely she's applying for art courses, not engineering or sciences? I would have expected you to be going to very different universities." He said, bewildered.

"I was hoping we would both go here." She admitted in the same quiet voice. "My parents said I had to stay local if I wanted to go this year but I didn't want to stay for sixth year. All my friends are leaving."

"Is this because you're younger than your friends?" she nodded. "And your parents don't think you are mature enough to live on your own in another part of the country?" again she nodded.

"Okay, and your friend got accepted elsewhere I'm assuming?" The nods were getting annoying but it was the only answer he was getting.

"You know, people often drift apart after high school. It's a fact of life. If she feels that she would be better off at a different university, perhaps you need to let her. She may resent you if you try to hold her back." He said gently. "And if she's a good friend then she will keep in touch. You can see her during the holidays and talk over the internet."

Anne sniffed. "S'not fair." she mumbled. "I don't want to lose her."

The teacher was at a loss, having expected a talk about grades and university applications. He was a bit out of his depth now that it had devolved to tears.

"Tell you what, check the postings just now." she did and the offers were up.

"I got all my offers." she said, tearfully.

He sighed. "Okay, wait here."

He went back into the class and retrieved her belongings. "Okay class, revise quietly for a bit, I just have to go to the office for a minute or two."

He came back out and led Anne down the stairs. "Okay, do you know where Miss Rosenberg is just now?"

She nodded, "English Literature with Mrs Boyde."

"Okay, let's go have a chat." They walked in silence across the empty school. Stopping down the corridor from the English classroom. "Wait here a minute."

He strode to the door and knocked. "Mrs Boyde, may I speak with young Miss Rosenberg for a few minutes?" There was an audible chorus of "Oooo!" from the students before the teacher hushed them.

"What's wrong?" Abby asked as she left the class.

"Nothing Miss Rosenberg, I just wanted to sit down for a few minutes with yourself and my student over there and discuss some things rationally." Abby noticed Anne standing down the hall for the first time and went pale.

"Is this about us going out?" she asked, sheepishly.

"No... though that does explain a few things. Come on, let's find a quiet place to talk." He led them up the stairs to the administration offices. "Helen, I'm just borrowing a meeting room for a few minutes." he called to the woman in the office, she waved him in.

"Now, first thing I guess Miss Rosenberg, would you like to check the offer postings? I believe you may find there is an offer waiting." he waited as Abby took out her phone and refreshed the page.

She sighed, "I got in."

"Now, we need to speak about why you are each going to this university, Miss Rosenberg, if I am correct you are a fairly prodigious artist?" He asked.

"I don't know if I would say prodigious! But yeah, I'm an artist." She said puzzled.

"And Anne here is a very intelligent scientist. Or, soon to be."

Abby closed her eyes, "And you think I shouldn't hold Anne back by making her go to the backwater local university?"

"Hmm, interesting." He said with a frown, "I had actually been thinking the opposite. There are a good many Universities with very highly coveted art courses."

"Yeah, but I never really wanted to go far. I always just sort of liked the idea of staying local." She looked at him seriously, "I'm more worried that Anne is staying here just to be with me."

"Well. I think this is actually much ado about nothing as Mrs Boyde might say." he chuckled, "As it turns out, Anne's parents have dictated the school she is to go to due to her tender age, unless of course, Anne is willing to wait until her majority. Which it appears she does not want to do!"

Abby looked up at Anne, "Really?" When she received a nod in response Abby got out of her seat and tackled Anne in a hug. "Oh my god, I have been so worried ever since the mid-year results came out. I thought I was holding you back!"

The teacher smiled, "You may not be but her parents certainly are. That said, I think perhaps it may work out well. You can always do a postgraduate degree somewhere else." He stood up, "Now, I think perhaps you both may be able to study a little better so let's get back to class."

eee

Jo opened the door to her home and shouted, "I got it!" She ran up the corridor and hugged her mum. "I got it, I got it, I got it!" She swung her mum around in a circle. "I'm going to university!"

"I'm so proud of you Joanne." her mum said with a huge smile.

"I'm proud too Jo." Her dad said leaning on the kitchen door frame with a coffee mug in his hand. "I talked to Rick a few times. He made me realise how damned stupid I was being. Here's the financial stuff you need for your scholarship." He handed Jo a stack of papers. "I'm sorry for being an arse."

Jo looked at her mum who gave a little head shake. "Thanks, dad." She said, accepting the papers. "You know I will need these next year too?"

"Yeah. It's fine." He said, ruffling her hair. "Now, how about we treat you to takeaways? Anything you like."

ele

"So, you got all your applications accepted? Did Abby?" Pete asked when Anne had calmed down enough to talk.

"Yeah, she got into the art course." She said with a smile.

"Good, well that makes this investment worthwhile then." He said, fishing out a real estate pamphlet.

Anne grabbed the leaflet, it looked like the same building Susan had shown her. "Is this?" she asked, hardly daring to hope.

"Mine to lend you for a few years? Yes." He said, teasing her.

"No! Is it the same building as Susan and Jo?" she said with some urgency.

"And the same floor even." He said and then had to cover his ears to protect from the squealing. Anne gave her dad a bone-crushing hug and then did the same for her mum.

"I'm going to Abby's" she called, not waiting for a response before running to the door.

⁓ℓℓ⁓

Mae called Heather's phone, "Please tell me you got in?"

"Of course I did, did you?" she asked in return.

"Of course. Guess who also got in?" She asked cheekily before a new voice came on the line.

"I did it, Heather!"

"Lucia? Oh my god! We're all going to the same uni!" Heather said in excitement, "Oh I can't wait to tell Susan!"

Mae was jumping up and down on her bed in excitement.

"Honey, don't jump on your bed, you're not four years old anymore!" her mum called from downstairs. "Did you tell Heather about the flat?"

"Heather, my dad has rented us a flat, it has three bedrooms! Want to see if your parents will let you rent a room?"

⁓ℓℓ⁓

On Saturday there was a definite feeling of celebration, Pete was running the pizza oven, chatting with Susan and Heather whilst the other girls chatted inside.

Heather was drinking a beer which Pete had offered her, knowing she was now eighteen. "So, to friends?" he said, raising his glass.

"To friends!" the two girls toasted. "And to cool flats like they had in friends!" Heather added.

"Yeah, thanks Pete. I promise we won't abuse your trust. It was super cool you doing that for Anne." Susan said with a smile.

"Hey, we were the ones insisting she stay local. I'm just amazed her friends all did too."

"You know Anne is the most mature and responsible one of all our friends? Except perhaps Jo." Susan asked, "I'm pretty sure she would have managed to survive anywhere."

"Well, now we won't have to worry if that would have been the case." He said with a smile, "And even better, you can all still come and have movie nights and pizza here once a month!"

Heather was sent away again with a cooked pizza and Susan turned to Pete. "You know, I'm glad our okay with me and Jo being an item. Anne says if it had been a boy I was seeing there would be no way I would be allowed a sleepover with him."

Pete frowned, "Yeah, I don't know, it's different. But I do trust you Susan, and I really like Jo which helps a lot."

"So if it were Abby I was seeing?" she joked.

"Oh hell no! It would be six feet of separation at all times!" he laughed.

"I don't think she's so bad." Susan said contemplatively, "And you must trust her a fair bit, allowing her to flat with Anne."

"Well, yes. She's not so bad. She was a bad influence sometimes when they were growing up though. I think she's matured, and it's not like I see her out chasing boys, and I doubt she will keep Anne up all night drinking." he admitted.

"Yes, I certainly have never seen her chasing the boys!" Susan laughed.

It was far later than normal when the girls moved upstairs, Heather had left her backpack in Anne's room due to the three bottles of sparkling wine it contained and she was trying to climb the ladder one-handed and not clink the bottles together.

When she got to the top and unloaded the bag Kelly saw the bottles and exclaimed "Wine! Can I have some?"

Heather looked to Anne for confirmation.

"She's thirteen Heather!" Anne proclaimed.

"One glass wouldn't hurt." Heather assured her.

Anne gave her a death glare whilst Kelly was making puppy dog eyes. "Half a glass," She relented, "and you sip it!"

"You thought we would get into trouble for drinking? If mum saw us giving Kelly wine we would be done for!" Anne assured them.

They settled in to watch the movie, Abby and Anne enjoying being able to snuggle up together without having to hide their relationship.

"Man, I wish I had someone to cuddle with!" Mae complained, seeing the two couples.

"You can cuddle me!" Kelly told her.

"Not quite the same but good enough." Mae accepted and she snuggled in beside Kelly.

Abby couldn't understand why but the girls all seemed to enjoy the movie. She hated it, cringing all the way through. She also didn't notice Mae sneaking more wine into Kelly's glass.

It was already fairly late when the film ended but people were getting used to the double features so Anne put on Conan the Barbarian. Kelly was already asleep on Mae's shoulder.

Mae and Heather were the only ones who seemed to be drinking, Abby and Anne had a couple of glasses each but Heather seemed to be well in her cups, making lewd comments about Arnold Schwarzenegger and getting quite loud.

"Heather, remember the conversation about being quiet and not letting my parents know we were drinking?" Anne asked her tactfully.

"Yeah! Duh!" Heather said loudly.

"Well, at the moment you are being quite loud...you know... the opposite of quiet?"

"Oh!" Heather said, nodding sagely, "Shhhhhhhhhh." she winked.

Kelly took that moment to wake, "Mmm, I love you Mae. I wish you were a lesbian so I could kiss you."

Anne looked around, "Oh for fuck sake! Mae, have you been feeding Kelly wine?" Mae looked sheepish. "Well, drunk Kelly is your responsibility. No more wine. For anyone!"

She took the wine bottles away and realised there was only a glass remaining in the last bottle. "Okay, scratch that, Abby and I will finish the wine."

"Don't kiss my sister!" Anne hissed at Mae who apparently was locking tongues with the thirteen-year-old. "Right, that's it, Kelly, over there, Mae, the other side of the room."

"Oh come on, it was only a bit of fun, we weren't serious!" Mae complained, moving away.

"I think I preferred the quiet Mae, I think Lucia is corrupting you." Anne lamented.

Susan and Jo were smiling, not lifting a hand to help.

Fortunately, there were no further drunken shenanigans before the end of the film and Heather, Mae, Jenny and Kelly were all fast asleep by the end of the movie. Heather was snoring quite loudly.

"Sorry guys," Anne whispered, "You can use my bed if you like. I would offer Kelly's but her room is disgusting."

They all snuck downstairs, brushing their teeth in the bathroom. "Next time, we are not doing this in my parent's house!" Anne said emphatically.

Susan and Jo disappeared into Anne's bedroom to avoid the snoring and Anne looked at Abby. "We could sleep on the couch?"

"Hey, I'm up for using Kelly's room, I don't care if it's a tip."

"It's not just a tip, it smells weird." Anne said, holding her nose.

"Yeah, but it's a real bed. Come on, let's just use it." Anne relented and they slipped into Kelly's room. It wasn't actually as bad as the last time Anne had been in it. It was still a tip, in fact, they had to move numerous things off the bed just so they could get in, but it didn't smell too bad.

They slipped under the rainbow unicorn covers and Abby sniggered, "You know, that's us? Apparently, they call lesbians who realise they are gay and have never slept with a man a unicorn?"

"What, that's dumb." Anne replied. "Anyway, I think they would more accurately call us virgins! It's not like we've had sex."

"We could resolve that issue, you know." Abby said, snuggling her neck.

They didn't but they got pretty darned close.

The next morning, after a significant amount of snuggle time, the girls got out of Kelly's nice soft bed to find three very hungover girls still trying to sleep it off upstairs.

"Where's Jenny?" Abby asked them. According to the grunts and groans, they figured she had gone down for breakfast.

"Kelly, if mum asks, you were not drinking last night and you are not hungover right? Do you understand me?" she got a vague yes from the bottom of the sleeping bag. Apparently, she had decided to crawl in headfirst after visiting the toilet during the night.

"And Mae..." she looked at the girl and shook her head, deciding against berating her.

"Just, try not to look too hungover when you come down? There are headache pills in the bathroom cupboard." she said and left them to sleep.

They greeted Anne's father downstairs, joining in the ritual paper read.

"Late night last night?" Pete asked, knowing the answer.

"Yeah, pretty late." Anne answered.

"Slept in Kelly's bed?" He casually asked.

"Yeah, mine was occupied." Anne replied, trying to stay casual. "And Heather was snoring like a freight train."

"Yes, we heard." Pete said, knowingly. "You and Abby looked fairly... comfortable."

Anne looked at Abby and took a deep breath, "Yeah?" she said, her voice coming out a little squeaky.

"Something I should know?"

"Nope, no, not really." Anne replied instantly.

"Hmm..." he said, looking over his non-existent glasses, "Is that so?" Anne nodded furiously.

Pete breathed a sigh. "I wasn't born yesterday, but I'm not going to push it. If there hypothetically were something going on, I would not stop you from moving in together. Just so you know." He returned to reading the paper.

"Me and Abby have been dating since last year." Anne blurted.

"Hmm." Pete said, continuing to read his paper.

Anne looked at Abby who shrugged. "Sorry." She said, casting her eyes downward.

"What are you sorry for?" Pete asked, looking at her again.

"Not telling you." she mumbled.

"Hmm." he nodded and returned to his paper.

Anne looked again at her girlfriend, her face crinkling up. "Dad?" she squeaked.

He looked at her and laughed, "Oh come here! I was just winding you up. Come on." He hugged her close. "I don't mind you didn't tell me. It's a big thing and I'm glad I know." He held his other arm open for Abby and she came in to join the hug. "Now, can I tell your mother?" Anne nodded into his neck.

Jenny was smiling like a lunatic at the display.

They said nothing as Jane came in a few minutes later, the scene having returned to a normal Sunday morning. They finished their breakfast quietly reading until the three hungover girls appeared, bleary-eyed and shuffling.

"Didn't sleep well?" Pete asked them, they gladly accepted this excuse and Kelly poured them all a glass of milk.

Pete timed it so that both Kelly and his wife were taking drinks and said, "So, it turns out Kelly's your only hope for grandchildren now dear." Before smiling into his mug as he took a drink.

Kelly almost lost milk out of her nose, Jane however was far more poised, she simply paused with the cup at her lips for several seconds before swallowing and saying. "I think you may find that boat sailed dear. Kelly told me some time ago that she is batting for the other team."

Apparently squirting hot coffee out of your nose is far less pleasant than milk.

EPILOGUE

I t was going to be the first movie night in their new flats, for some reason Anne and Abby didn't own a TV, Anne claimed it was because her dad wanted them to go home to her parents house once a month for movie night but whatever the reason, it meant movie night was at Susan and Jo's house this time.

Jo was finding that hosting a party was oddly stressful, they had clubbed together and ordered pizza but even without having to cook the flat had to be clean, the beds made, well, the one bed. Jo had never actually slept in hers yet, the only use it saw was during the... christening of the flat. Needless to say, there were only four rooms really, the kitchen was open plan off the living room and so it hadn't taken them long, it was almost fully christened the first day! God what a day.

They had moved the sofa from the other girls flat for the night so now they had three two seaters in a horseshoe shape. It was a bit cramped, you had to climb over the arm of a chair to visit the loo but it worked, and it was so much more grown up than beanbags on the floor. Jo smiled thinking back to that first movie night watching Rocky Horror. It seemed wrong not having invited Kelly, she had actually been instrumental in getting Susan and her together, something she was never planning on telling Susan but the paper picked out of the bag had been Kelly's, Jo had also written the same film and had accidentally taken credit when Susan asked. It had come up the next morning but it seemed a bit late to admit to Susan, it seemed especially late months later when her girlfriend admitted it had been a big decider when she was thinking of asking her out.

Realising there were no large bowls in the flat that they could put snacks in Joe grabbed the keys to the other flat from the hook.

"I'm off to borrow some bowls from Anne!" She called out to her girlfriend who was lounging in the tub. "Back soon."

The flats were honest to God across from each other, just like in friends. It was the greatest thing, having friends close, they had shared keys the first night and pretty much treated each other's flats as an extension of their own, a good thing considering one flat was missing a TV!

She unlocked the door and called out, "hey, anyone home." There was no answer so she just swung the door shut and stepped into the weirdly empty feeling flat. Anne was a neat freak so the flat was so tidy that they easily could have had the party here, without anyone tidying. As she was rooting about in the kitchen cupboard she realised she could hear something, she stopped and listened, bowls in hand and then she worked out what she was hearing! Sex. It was obviously escalating to erm... climax by the moans and screams. Jo tiptoed towards the front door, not wanting to disturb them, or to have the embarrassment of having them know she heard! Just as she reached the front door she heard what was obviously Anne's voice, "Oh god, don't fucking stop!" And then what sounded like a very passionate moan. Jo bit her lip to stop herself from laughing and she carefully let herself out, making sure to be as silent as possible.

When she got back to her flat Susan was making a cup of coffee, "That was quick, were they not in?"

"Oh, they were in all right, in bed, fucking like rabbits!" Jo sidled up to her girlfriend who was only wearing a silky robe. "Perhaps it's that time of the day?" She asked sliding her hand up under the short robe to caress the smooth bum underneath.

"I thought you said Anne wasn't into sex?" Susan asked, not allowing Jo to distract her from the espresso machine.

"I suspect they worked that out. It certainly sounded like she was enjoying it this afternoon!" She lent in to kiss Susan's neck.

"Oh crap, I have a feeling my coffee is going to get cold." Susan sighed as she turned and allowed Jo to gather her mouth in a steamy kiss, "I suspect you are a bit of a voyeur!" She accused her, not letting it stop the intimacy.

"What can I say, it sounded fun." She lifted Susan onto the kitchen counter and enthusiastically made use of Susan's squeaky clean body.

Susan's coffee went cold, even though it was inches from her hand at all times.

The other four girls arrived just after six pm, their flat was about a ten minute walk away but they had asked to use the 'spare' rooms for the night. Jo was a little despondent when she saw Jenny had a large collection of alcoholic drinks with her.

"At least my sister isn't here for Mae to corrupt this time!" Anne said, eyeing the bottles as they were set on the counter, "And at least it's not my flat!" This drew a groan from Jo.

"It's funny, my mum thinks it's all of you who will be corrupting me!" Lucia said, she had stopped wearing the headscarf as soon as her mum had left their flat and hadn't been to a mosque since then either. "She thinks all you four are doing is having lesbian sex all day. It's so funny."

Susan and Jo shared an amused glance, then turned to see the other couple decidedly pink.

"Well, she needn't concern herself with us corrupting you, we all have partners. It's Mae who is so desperate she gets a thirteen year old drunk and sucks face with her!" Susan quipped.

"It was just us messing around, we weren't serious!" Mae was a decided beetroot colour and seemed to be trying to make the far away couch consume her.

"Tell that to my sister, she still talks about that magnificent first kiss!" Anne said, continuing the ribbing. "I'm pretty sure there would have been another lesbian couple if I hadn't stopped them."

"Perhaps I should sleep in your room tonight Heather?" Lucia suggested.

"Hell no! I'm plying Mae with drink and having a drunken lesbian romp. Experimenting with my sexuality is an important part of the university experience!" Heather said extravagantly, causing the girls all to burst out laughing.

"Can we stop making fun of me now, please?" Mae begged.

They watched predator, almost every time Arnold was on screen someone did an impression, most were from different films. Mae almost constantly made the predator noise which got really annoying after about thirty seconds.

In all it was a success, most of the girls were drinking and the night was getting rowdy. The pizza arrived shortly after the film finished, Anne having calculated the movie timing and ordered before they started the film.

Susan saw Abby sneak next door and nodded to Jo, ushering her out to go have words.

Reluctantly Jo followed her, catching her friend rummaging in the fridge. "Hey." She started, scaring the shit out of Abby.

"Woh! I was not expecting you Jo!" She said with her hand on her heart.

"Yeah, about that. I think perhaps we need chains or something on the front doors."

Abby looked confused, "why?"

"Let's just say you might not want us barging in on you being intimate... again." Abby's face went slack.

"Oh no, you heard that?"

"Yeah, I'm guessing you sorted your problems with Anne?" Jo asked, sitting at the breakfast bar.

Abby sighed, "Not exactly."

"So what I heard today wasn't her having the most earth shattering orgasm?"

Abby blushed and looked at the counter, "It was but... it takes something special. Like, the planets have to align and the mood has to be exactly right. When that happens, whooee! God it's good."

"So, how often do you...?" Jo tried to put the words together and failed.

"Twice." Abby admitted with a tiny smile.

"Twice! You've been going out for a year! We did it more than that the first day we moved in! That must be really hard."

"Oh, no! That's just Anne, I mean, as long as I instigate she loves actually having sex and its sooo good. We have sex a lot but it always stops after me, she just kind of, likes the act but doesn't get to the point of erm... climax." Abby was looking ridiculously embarrassed. "The first time it actually happened she almost bit my clit off! I don't think she had ever expected it and geez it was so sexy, I kind of understand why she's happy to just please me you know? She honestly went limp afterwards, like she had no strength left."

"So she never starts anything?" Jo asked, steering the conversation away from the uncomfortable mechanics of the act.

"Well, she starts the kissing, hell I think if she had her way we would like our lives with our lips locked together. Honestly anywhere, the cinema, university, last night she gave me the most intense kiss standing right in the middle of the supermarket!" Jo smiled at this image. "It's just, if it were up to her it would never go past that. And often we don't, we just sit and kiss on the couch, and it's nice, intimate."

"Well, I'm glad you found out what works." Jo said and came around the counter to give Abby a hug. "But I'm getting a chain, we had just finished when you two walked in today and let's just say you would have gotten an eye full, we weren't exactly in the bedroom!"

Abby laughed and slapped Jo's arm, "I thought you looked a bit flustered when we came in!"

They returned to Jo's flat to find most of the pizza gone, "Jo! Play us a song Jo!" Jenny called as they walked in, obviously well in her cups.

"After a slice of pizza, you gannets would eat it all otherwise!" She said, grabbing a slice of pepperoni.

"Anne, next time can we invite your sister? I like her." Mae slurred. The girls all laughed at this. "What? She's nice and cuddly."

"Mae, are you sure your not gay?" Jenny asked her.

"I'm..." there was a long pause as Mae tried to think of the word, "Omnisexual, I love everyone!"

pliance